DOROTHY M. JOHNSON TITLES
AVAILABLE IN BISON BOOKS EDITIONS

Buffalo Woman
The Hanging Tree
Indian Country

All the Buffalo Returning

Dorothy M. Johnson

University of Nebraska Press

Lincoln

⊗ The paper in this book meets the minimum requirements of American National Standard for Information Sciences—Permanence of Paper for Printed Library Materials, ANSI Z39.48-1984.

First Bison Books printing: 1996
Most recent printing indicated by the last digit below:
10 9 8 7 6 5 4 3 2 1

Library of Congress Cataloging-in-Publication Data
Johnson, Dorothy M.
All the buffalo returning / Dorothy M. Johnson.
p. cm.
Sequel to Buffalo woman.
Summary: A Fictionalized account of the changing fortunes of the Hunkpapa and Oglala Sioux from the victory at the Battle of the Little Bighorn in 1876 to the massacre at Wounded Knee in 1890.
ISBN 0-8032-7590-0 (pa: alk. paper)
1. Hunkpapa Indians—Fiction. 2. Oglala Indians—Fiction.
3. Indians of North America—Fiction. [1. Hunkpapa Indians—Fiction. 2. Oglala Indians—Fiction. 3. Indians of North America—Fiction.] I. Title.
PS3519.O233A78 1996
[Fic]—dc20
95-43539 CIP
AC

Reprinted from the original 1979 edition by Dodd, Mead & Company, New York.

THIS BOOK IS FOR LILLIAN HORNICK

Contents

PART IV—1889
THE MESSIAH IS ON EARTH!

PART V—1890
THE EARTH WILL SHUDDER

PART I

THE GRANDMOTHER'S LAND

1877

EARLY SPRING 1877

THE HUNKPAPA FAMILY

ELK RISING, 36

BRINGS HORSES, 32, wife of Elk Rising, daughter of the late Whirlwind Woman

STORMY, 8, son of Brings Horses and Elk Rising

RED PIPE GIRL, 5, daughter of Brings Horses and Elk Rising

BLUE ROCK WOMAN, 27, wife of Elk Rising

BEAVER, 3, sickly son of Blue Rock and Elk Rising

WHITE MOUNTAIN, 21, brother of Elk Rising

STANDING TREE, 17, adopted son of Elk Rising

THE OGLALA FAMILY

MORNING RIDER, 36, son of the late Whirlwind Woman

YOUNG BIRD, 32, wife of Morning Rider

ANGRY, 12, Young Bird's son by a previous marriage

REACHES FAR GIRL, 8, daughter of Young Bird and Morning Rider

KILLS GRIZZLY (formerly called SHOOTS), 13, son of Morning Rider by a previous marriage

(SHE THROWS HIM, infant son of Morning Rider and the late Round Cloud Woman, is with another family temporarily)

1

‖‖‖‖‖‖‖‖‖‖‖‖‖‖‖‖‖‖‖‖‖‖‖‖‖‖‖‖‖

The Buffalo Will Always Be

The country through which they were riding was strange to the people, but they and their grandfathers' grandfathers had traveled in new territories and lived in them and felt at home there. As they moved on north, the snow became thinner on the ground; the grass was the pale green of coming spring under the sun.

Behind them they left death and disaster. With them, of no weight at all on the backs of the gaunt ponies, they carried their wounds, their grief, and their hope. They were riding away from death, moving north toward life.

One of the wise old men at the head of the column began to sing in a thin voice:

> "The earth lives, the earth lives.
> The earth lives. It is our mother."

Seventeen-year-old Standing Tree, riding today in spite of the pain of broken ribs, took up the song in his strong young man's voice: "The earth lives. It is our mother."

Behind them, miles behind them, in the branches of a great tree, was the gaunt body of Whirlwind Woman, wrapped in a ragged blanket. In her lifeless arms was the light body of her infant grandson. The arms of Brings Horses Woman, the child's mother, the dead woman's daughter, were empty now.

The old woman and her tiny grandson were traveling the Spirit Road together across the stars. "He is very young to travel the Spirit Road alone," Whirlwind had said. "I can find it. I will carry him to the far country in my arms."

And so she would, Brings Horses had no doubt. To the Land of Many Lodges, where lived all those who had gone before them, in stout buffalo-hide lodges with plenty of meat.

I still have two fine children—thin from hunger, but well—and my good, brave, strong man, Brings Horses remembered. We are all thin and ragged and cold, and many of us are wounded—but the earth lives; it is our mother.

She heard a bird sing and her heart leaped. She had forgotten, almost, what joy was. She glanced ahead, saw that her son Stormy and her daughter Red Pipe Girl were all right on their horses. She guided her horse out of line so as to ride beside her young brother-in-law, White Mountain, who had to lie on a pony drag because of the wound in his hip.

He smiled up at her and said, "Today we will get there, or tomorrow. I feel it."

There was some excitement up ahead, and Brings Horses hurried back to her place in the column, just behind her children, where she could watch them. At a shouted signal, everybody stopped. The warriors who were riding far out, watching, galloped in with their weapons ready.

Two of the *akícitas,* the messengers, who had been scouting far ahead were returning, flat to their horses' backs, making signs of gladness, not danger.

One of them yelled, "The piles of stones are just ahead. We saw them!"

Everyone began to shout, "The Grandmother's Land! We are almost there!"

But in spite of the excitement and the stirring, they waited while the *akícitas* reported formally to the old men, the chiefs. Not until these men gave the signal did the column move north again, with everyone staring, sending their sight as far as it would go to catch the piles of stones that marked the Medicine Line.

Strange, the power that was in those heaps of stones! The prairie looked just the same on both sides, but north of the stone piles the people would be safe from the Americans, from the soldiers in blue coats, who had fought so long and hard to kill them. To the north was the Grandmother's Land, ruled by a great woman chief far away across a big water.

The people kicked the ribs of their gaunt horses and passed between two stone heaps. When everyone was through and on safe ground, Blue Rock Woman gulped for air and said quietly, "Now we can breathe deep. I had almost forgotten how."

Blue Rock, like Brings Horses, was wife to Elk Rising. She looked down at the sick child on her arm—three years old, but very thin and weak. "Now we can take good care of you and you will get well," she told him, but he did not answer.

There was happy murmuring among all the people: Ah, a lovely valley! Right by a river for good water. . . . Good new grass for the pony herd. . . . Plenty of wood.

Without needing any orders, they began to unload the packhorses so the lodges would be in the proper order in that gracious, sheltering valley. Girls ran to bring firewood. Boys let the thin ponies drink their fill and then drove them up to find tender grass.

Men gathered to discuss the problems of defense and hunting.

Now there was the sound of a small drum and two old men singing: "The earth lives. The earth is our mother."

Two boys, who had taken a bunch of horses to graze, came running back to report to their father, "Two hunters coming with meat!"

There was much buzzing about this news; it was well that the boys brought it, so that the people were not alarmed when the two strange Indians rode into camp, each leading a packhorse with a fresh-killed deer loaded across its back. The two boys brought Chief Four Horns to meet them. They told him their names, and he shook hands with them, trusting them, for they plainly came as friends.

They spoke the same language, the Lakota tongue; like the newcomers, the hunters were of the great, scattered nation that the Wasichus, the whites, called Sioux. The Lakotas, the Sioux of the prairie, considered themselves the Real People, and their nation consisted of several divisions, but they were all one folk although the divisions had different names.

"We are Brulés," the older hunter said. "Our camp is that way," pointing.

"We are Hunkpapas and some Oglalas," Four Horns told them. "We have had a hard time. Especially the Oglalas. They lost lives and goods in a fight with the American soldiers."

"The Grandmother's country is a good place," the younger of the strangers told him. "We are glad to be here. The Red Coats speak with straight tongues. Your people are hungry, maybe? You have not had time to hunt?"

"We have just arrived," the old chief answered, "and the people have been hungry for a long time. The Blue Coats attacked the Oglalas, killed many, destroyed much. Since then, the Oglalas have been with us."

The older stranger said, "My son will leave his deer with you."

The listening men murmured thanks and admiration for this generosity, and the women cried for joy while they ran forward with their knives to butcher the deer carcass. After another handshake, the hunters rode on.

Girls and grandmothers built up the cooking fires and set the cooking pots to boiling even before the lodges were ready to move into. Raw meat was good, but cooked meat with freshly dug roots in the soup made more for everyone to eat.

Then down by the river Brings Horses and another woman, dipping up water, saw something and screamed with terror; they ran back to the lodges. The people's happiness and hope were shattered by fear. Boys came pelting back with the horses. Women began to tear down their lodges again. Small children, running free, shrieked and sought their mothers. For right across the river two men sat their horses, one man who looked Indian and another who was plainly a soldier chief although they could not tell whether his uniform was blue, because his coat of fur concealed it.

The people were not safe, after all. Behind those two men there might be a whole army, hidden now by a butte. Old Four Horns shouted a command to his fighting men, but it was not really needed. Every Lakota warrior seized his weapons and his shield and ran to stand on the river bank at the shallow fording place, facing the enemy.

The two men made the sign for peace, but who could believe them? The white man spoke to his companion, who shouted in Lakota, "We come in peace," and fired his rifle into the air. An empty gun meant the same as the words: We come in peace.

Could they believe that? There was silence, almost, and then two more Indians came galloping from behind the butte to join the strangers.

Now the women were more alarmed than ever. They picked up their children and ran toward the sheltering hills.

The white man leaped off his horse and flung off his fur coat. There he stood, wearing the scarlet coat of the Grandmother's police, those men who spoke with a straight tongue.

He and his scouts stayed on their side of the river, and one of his half-Indians interpreted for him. The Red Coat mounted again and approached the ford, but the desperate Lakotas threatened with guns and bows. He shouted, explaining, and his scout kept telling the Lakotas his words in their own language: "We will not hurt you. I speak for the Queen, for Grandmother England. I want to talk to your chief."

The Lakotas could not help admiring his courage and his patience. When he rode across the ford there were arrows aimed at his heart, but he gave no sign of fear.

Four Horns—seventy years old, but straight backed and commanding—rode toward him. The two men leaned forward on their horses and shook hands.

The women returned cautiously, some with tears of relief on their cheeks, and went back to work while the men talked.

Through his scout interpreter, the white man said, "I am Major James Walsh. I serve the Queen. When you can gather your subchiefs and other head men, I will tell you the orders she has for all of you who come from the United States. All Indians who have come here already follow these laws, and all those who will come after you. Sitting Bull is not with you, I think."

Old Four Horns said, "He is my nephew and adopted son. He is still south of the Missouri River, but I think he will come here. Major Walsh, you are tired. You have ridden far today? Would you like to rest?"

Walsh was, in fact, exhausted, for he had traveled very far, patrolling the Medicine Line, supervising his handful of scattered uniformed constables. He said, "I would like to rest. Then I will talk to all your people."

They found him a good lodge, and he went sound asleep in it, totally relaxed on a buffalo robe. That made great, admiring talk all through the camp: "The Red

Coat, Walsh, is not afraid of anyone. He lay down and went to sleep. He trusts us!"

Four Horns sent boys all through the camp with a message: "When the lodges are set up and the people have eaten a little food, then everybody will come to hear the words of the Grandmother's red-coat chief. Everybody! Women and children too."

They hurried with the work they had to do, while their hearts sang. They were safe across the border! Then they went to sit in front of the lodge where Major Walsh slept, the men in front, the women and children behind them. In the lodges a few old women stayed to tend the fires and look after some of the wounded who were too exhausted to come to the meeting.

White Mountain, hip-wounded, was so low in spirit that he intended to sit with the women. He knew he would never again be agile enough, swift-moving enough, to fight like a man. But four members of his warrior society came for him, all walking, leading a horse with a pony drag. They laughed at him, joked as friends joke who have been through bad times together, lifted him quickly and gently onto the pony drag, and walked beside him to the big council. They remembered to take along a backrest from a bed. They made him comfortable in his proper place among the young warriors.

All the people were attentive and silent. Even the children were quiet. The interpreter, Lavallie, who had been born of a French father and a Lakota mother, asked Four Horns, "Are they all here now?"

"All who can come," the old chief told him. "A few wounded are in the lodges, a few old women to keep the fires burning."

So Lavallie entered the lodge and spoke to the sleeping Walsh, who came out to look at the people and to speak, with pauses for Lavallie to interpret into their language.

"Do you all understand," he asked, "that you are now on British soil, in the land of the Queen?"

Four Horns answered, "We know that. We all know."

Major Walsh continued: "We have laws here that everyone must obey—Indians, white men, everyone. You must obey them or go back to where you came from.

"You must not kill anyone.

"You must not steal anything.

"You must not injure any person or anything that belongs to him.

"All men must protect all women and children. This is our most sacred law.

"Your men must not cross the Medicine Line to take horses or harm any Americans.

"If you obey these laws, you are safe, you can sleep at night. We will protect you here. But if you break them, you must go back."

The audience hardly breathed. It was good to have the laws made clear, the same laws for everyone, not laws that changed at the whim of every Wasichu who wanted to kill an Indian!

Old Four Horns held out his hand to Walsh. "We are tired. We have been pursued and attacked. Our women and children cry for rest. All we ask is peace and a chance to hunt for buffalo. We take your words into our hearts."

There was an audible sigh of relief among the listening women. They had come to a land of peace at last! Now, Brings Horses Woman thought, our children can run

11

and play again as children should, without always having to wonder whether a Wasichu will kill them! Now we need not keep looking over our shoulders all the time for blue-coat soldiers.

The strong-faced man in the red coat spoke again, and his interpreter translated:

"I have something else important to tell you. My Queen has her own Indians, who have always lived on this side of the Medicine Line, even before there was such a line. They do not like to have your people here, or the other Indians who have come from the United States. But you must not fight with them, and I will punish them if they try to fight with you. Do you understand?"

Four Horns made the sign of agreement. "We understand that. But we belong to the Grandmother, too."

"No," said Walsh. "That is not the way it is. Sometimes game is scarce, because now there are too many hunters here. If the Queen's Indians are hungry, she will feed them. But you and your people are not her children. You may live and hunt here as long as you obey her laws and can support yourselves. But if the buffalo herds fail and your people are hungry, my Queen will not give you rations. You will have to go back to the United States."

All of them had heard about that threat from Lakotas who had been in Canada and had come back to the south to tell about it, but they did not want to believe. A murmur like a groan came from the audience. Four Horns made the hand sign that says, "My heart is on the ground."

There was a stirring. An Indian came from behind the rest, a Lakota, and leaped from his horse and pushed through the crowd of seated people until he was up front, facing Major Walsh. He shook hands with Chief Four Horns, then pointed at Walsh and accused him: "You are a spy from the camp of Bear Coat. I saw you there once! You are an American!"

There was a gasp from the people, and the men grasped their weapons.

Walsh answered his accuser: "You are a spy yourself. I am no spy for Colonel Miles, the man you call Bear Coat, or for anyone else. You are no friend of the people of Four Horns or you would not disturb them with such lies. You have a bad heart."

Everything good was undone now. The refugees were suspicious and afraid. Walsh was one against many, but he was a brave man. He turned to Four Horns.

"Will your people be easier in their minds if I stay overnight?"

The chief signed "Yes."

"Then I ask you to keep that traitor from running away while you send a message for me. Send two or three of your young men, and I will pay them. Very far from here, in the United States, Medicine Bear and Black Horn and their people are camping. I want your young men to ride and tell them that you have here as a prisoner White Forehead, chief of the country north of the Medicine Line."

Four Horns objected. "White Forehead is not a prisoner."

"I *am* a prisoner. If I try to get away, your warriors will stop me. Use that word 'prisoner' in the message."

Four Horns appointed four riders, and Walsh and his handful of half-Indian scouts slept in the camp that night, with an Indian guard at the door of the lodge to protect them. The people of Four Horns, alarmed and bewildered, did not sleep so well.

Two days later Walsh was relieved to hear a war whoop down the valley. The two men he had sent for—chiefs of the Yankton Lakotas—were coming—with two hundred of their fighting men behind them, galloping, yelling, their eagle feathers and fringes flying, all the men brandishing their weapons and coup sticks.

First to arrive was Black Horn. He pulled his horse to a sliding stop, leaped off, and ran to embrace Major Walsh like a brother. Right behind him was Medicine Bear, who did the same.

Black Horn demanded of Four Horns, "What man says White Forehead is an American? That man is a liar and I want him." The accuser had managed to sneak away and escape from the camp.

Medicine Bear admonished, "If you people want to live here, you must obey the law as White Forehead tells you."

Black Horn added, "We came ready for war, but our hearts are glad to find no reason for war. Listen to White Forehead. His talk is straight. We have come to live here. Our families are coming behind us."

Walsh and his guides left that day for their post in the Cypress Hills. Before they departed, Four Horns had a sincere talk with Walsh. They smoked together in dignity and friendship, with the interpreter present, and Four Horns brought out several large silver medals strung on a buckskin cord.

"We have come home, White Forehead," he said earnestly, "to the protection of the Queen, our Grandmother. We were British Indians long ago. My grandfathers received these medals as tokens of friendship from your grandfathers. Your chief was a man then, not a woman, but our grandfathers fought on his side in long-ago wars against the Americans.

"Then the American Grandfather said we were his children, and the land where we hunted was his land. We do not know how this happened, but that is the way it was. So we are the Queen's Indians and we will live here where the laws are just.

"Many of our men have medals like these, proving that their grandfathers fought on the side of your great chief who lives across the big water. We would have showed you before but that man interrupted and caused trouble. He got away—I am sorry. We are your Indians, and we have come home to live."

Walsh, White Forehead, replied, "No, you belong to your own Grandfather, chief of the United States. That is the law."

"The man who claims to be our grandfather hates us. We must live where the hunting is no good, he says, on a reservation in a place called Dakota. If we live there, we starve and die. If we will not live there, he sends his soldiers to kill us.

"We know what it is like there, because many of our people have tried to live there. Some of them ran away, because if they stayed they would starve. They suffered, so they escaped and came to join us. Do you know what happened when we were coming here for refuge?"

"I know," Walsh answered briefly. "The soldiers attacked the Oglala camp at night, killed some, wounded many, destroyed much goods. The Oglalas sent messengers to you. You saved them. If your people had not caught up with them by riding hard, all the Oglalas would have died on the prairie." He shook his head and said in sign, "My heart is on the ground.

"You can stay here as long as you obey the Queen's laws," he repeated, "and as long as you can feed yourselves by hunting. Then you must go back. I have spoken."

Four Horns took heart. "We are good hunters. The best. The buffalo have always been. The buffalo will always be! Wakan Tanka, the Great Mystery, gave them to us in numbers beyond counting. We will always have buffalo to hunt. That is how we live. Wakan Tanka wants us to live. We are his people. He made us."

2

"I Can Do Little Things"

The newcomers could not understand why the Grandmother across the big water rejected them as her children, but after the shock of learning this, they did not worry very much.

They remembered Fort Laramie, far to the south, where they used to trade. Past it went the Oregon Trail, with the constant stream of covered wagons and dirty Wasichus, always going westward, so many of them that the trail was thought to have some magic in it, to be able to produce so many. They called it the Medicine Road. Those people had ruined the hunting, because the road became so wide and dirty that no grass grew and the buffalo herds stopped crossing it. Here in Canada there was no Medicine Road to discourage the immense brown herds.

But it was very strange—the land was the same everywhere: Wakan Tanka, the Great Holy, had put them on it. Where did this boundary between nations come from, and why? A vague boundary between hunting territories they could understand very well, as when the Lakotas had pushed the Crows out of certain country long ago, fighting with them. But the Grandmother in England and the Grandfather in Washington were not fighting about anything. They were being very careful to avoid fighting, in fact, very polite to each other through their subchiefs. For both nations, the refugee Indians from the United States were a serious problem.

Four Horns' band of Hunkpapas and Oglalas had arrived in Canada in March. The wounded healed, the hunters brought back meat and hides, the women tanned the hides and made good new lodge covers. In the new land, after the shifting of the people was finished, Elk Rising the Hunkpapa had his lodge next to that of his wife's brother, Morning Rider the Oglala; and both were near that of Four Horns, uncle of Sitting Bull.

All of them were anxious for Sitting Bull to come, that great leader with strong medicine power.

These people belonged to the lodges of Grandmother Whirlwind's son and daughter:

THE OGLALA FAMILY

MORNING RIDER, Whirlwind's son
YOUNG BIRD, his wife, with dreadful scars on her cheek and one side of her scalp where her hair had been burned off in the battle with the Wasichu soldiers
ANGRY, her son
KILLS GRIZZLY, son of Morning Rider and a mother now dead
REACHES FAR GIRL, daughter of Young Bird and Morning Rider
BROWN LEAF, wife of Morning Rider

At first Morning Rider had two young widows whom he had taken in after the battle. A good man, a widower, asked for one of them, and Morning Rider married the other, BROWN LEAF WOMAN.

Morning Rider's infant son, SHE THROWS HIM, had no mother; she had been killed by a blue-coat soldier in battle when the American soldiers attacked the people on the way to Canada. So the baby lived for the time being with another family, where a nursing mother had lost a baby during that awful time.

THE HUNKPAPA FAMILY

ELK RISING
BRINGS HORSES WOMAN, his wife, daughter of Whirlwind
STORMY, their son
RED PIPE GIRL, their daughter
BLUE ROCK WOMAN, another wife of Elk Rising
BEAVER, their sickly small son
WHITE MOUNTAIN, hip-wounded warrior brother of Elk Rising
STANDING TREE, adopted son of Elk Rising

All the people, except the babies too young to remember, lived with grief because of the loss of their loved ones. The most strong-hearted hid their grief and reached out with compassion to those visibly suffering.

Young Bird's burns were long in healing, and her scars were so ugly that she was ashamed. Therefore, her husband, Morning Rider, was more attentive to her than before, praising everything she did, and his sister, Brings Horses, kept reminding her that she was a heroine.

"You saved so many things from the lodge when it was burning!" she said. "You were so brave. Nobody will ever forget it. Even with your sister Round Cloud shot down before your eyes, you never lost your control. You thought of the needs of the family, of the people. You are a true Lakota!"

The little boy, She Throws Him, although he lived in another lodge, received much loving education from his father, Morning Rider, and his aunt, Brings Horses. Even before he could understand, they told him over and over the story of his grandmother and how he got his name. It was important that he know, that he remember to be proud. Brings Horses said:

"Whirlwind Woman was my mother, your father's mother, your grandmother. Her spirit has gone now to the Land of Many Lodges, where we all will go sometime. She died just before we came here, into the Queen's country. It was only a year ago that she saved your life. You were on your cradleboard, and she took you along when she went to dig roots. A grizzly bear came, an old-woman bear with a cub, and would have killed you. But Grandmother Whirlwind threw you and your cradleboard up high to safety from a gully, and the grizzly bear gouged a great chunk out of Whirlwind's leg with her claws. So Grandmother Whirlwind was sick for a long time and never walked again easily, as other people do. Your big brother killed the bear with arrows and his knife, although he had not yet gone out to lament to the spirits for medicine to protect him. That is how he got his name, Kills Grizzly. Your grandmother received an honorable name, too, bestowed by the great chief Crazy Horse himself. He gave her the name Saved Her Cub because of the brave thing she had done to save you.

"Just before she died, she gave her name to a baby younger than you. It was the last thing she owned to give away. That baby, my baby boy, is dead now. Grandmother Whirlwind took him with her to the Land of Many Lodges. They are happy there, and well.

"And you, my little man, little warrior, you must learn your own name. It is She Throws Him. That name was given to you in honor by Chief Crazy Horse too!"

Life went on. The brother of Elk Rising walked, at first with a staff and then without it, always with some pain, always with a limp. Sometimes White Mountain went to a place where he could be alone and prayed, telling the Great Mystery, "I give you my pain as an offering. I thank you for letting me live." He took along a small drum and sang his thanks.

Blue Rock Woman's ailing little boy never recovered from his winter sickness. He died before he was four years old. He was the only child she had, and her grief was pitiful.

The Lakotas who had come north before Four Horns' band came calling in family groups from time to time, bringing meat, looking for old friends, for relatives who had married into Hunkpapa and Oglala families, exchanging news. They were free as in the old days, not worried any more about blue-coat soldiers, not much worried about the Queen's Indians who did not want them there. The Queen's laws protected everybody, and White Forehead and his men enforced them with justice and punishment for those who broke them.

In early May, Sitting Bull himself led the ragged, hungry remnants of his people across the Medicine Line, about forty lodges of them, and listened to the same lecture that his predecessors had received from Grandmother England's fearless red-coated Major Walsh.

Sitting Bull had never wanted to have anything to do with any Wasichu. He was the most respected chief among all the Lakotas, the man most feared by white men in the entire United States and Canada. He was not accustomed to being given orders. But when White Forehead told him how he and his people must act, he promised to follow the Queen's laws, to keep his young men north of the border, to keep the peace. He and Major Walsh even became friends. They had much in common: they were determined, they were strong leaders, they never showed fear or doubt.

Sitting Bull had his own ways of finding out what was happening to the Lakotas who had stayed in the United States. Two or three young men on good horses could always cross the border somewhere without being caught by Walsh's red-coat constables or half-blood scouts. Occasionally a few Indians escaped from the reservation in Dakota Territory, crossed the line, and sought refuge in Canada.

So the news came that on the same day Sitting Bull had led his hungry people past a stone pile into the Queen's country, Chief Crazy Horse of the Oglalas had surrendered to the Blue Coats.

When the messengers came with that news, Sitting

Bull called all the Lakota head men to a council to hear the report. In addition, he made sure that Major Walsh received the news accurately, not in some lying, twisted version that the Wasichus down south might send.

Sitting Bull held his council in a lodge with the cover rolled up all around so the people outside could see and hear—the warriors up close and the women just behind them, as many as could get within hearing distance.

They all knew the great and terrible fact already—it spread through all the lodges in all the camps like wind-driven fire through dry grass across the prairie.

But now they heard the details. Crazy Horse had fought the Wasichus; he had prayed long. He consulted his subchiefs. He had a long and private conversation with General Crook.

"I will get you a new reservation," General Crook had promised, "in good hunting country for your people. I will arrange it with the Grandfather in Washington. It is the best thing for you. There will be no more fighting, no more dead and wounded in battle. Your children will not go hungry any more."

Crazy Horse had listened to promises from the Wasichus' big chiefs, messages carried by his own Oglalas who had already surrendered at the agencies. Some of them were paid by the Wasichus now; they were Indian police and wore blue coats like the soldiers. They did what they must to protect their families. Some of the white men meant well. Some of them lied. General Crook meant well.

Red Cloud Agency was a mile from the soldier town, Fort Robinson, in Nebraska. That was where Crazy Horse and the last of the Lakota hostiles came. He and his head men rode in front. They wore warbonnets of nodding eagle plumes, but Crazy Horse, that strange, humble leader, wore no battle honors, only the eagle feather of a warrior on the back of his head.

Behind them rode the other warriors, and then came the rest of the Oglalas, men and women and children, and horses pulling travois and all the dogs cavorting around them.

They came like conquerors, singing a Lakota peace song. Crazy Horse's heart was on the ground (although his head was high). He would have torn it out with his fingernails, bleeding, if he had known he was leading his people to defeat and disaster and starvation.

Almost a thousand of the Oglalas came in and pitched their camp. The soldiers trained guns on them, made them give up their guns and all their horses. They were naked before men who hated them.

Crazy Horse counseled patience. General Crook had promised a good reservation, a place to hunt forever. But it would take some time. Wait a little. It takes time.

Sitting Bull, cooling himself in immense dignity with an eagle-wing fan, looked at the ground. "It will take more time than the earth endures," he said solemnly.

The people returned to their lodges, mourning.

In June the Lakotas in Canada came together, at the call of Sitting Bull and another Hunkpapa chief, Gall, in the sacred ceremony of the Sun-gazing Dance.

In this annual gathering of supplication and rejoicing, the people worshiped Wakan Tanka, the Great Mystery, as personified by the sun. And the spirit of the tribe itself was renewed for another year.

After slow and solemn ceremonies came the dance

itself, when men who had made vows to Wakan Tanka paid these vows with their own suffering. With sharpened sticks thrust through the skin of their chests or shoulders, and the sticks tied with thongs to heavy weights or a sacred tree, the men danced, staring at the sun, without food or water, until the skin and flesh tore loose and they fell and were free. They did this for the good of all the people.

But this year there were few men to pay with pain the vows they had made; many of them had died in battle. The finery they wore for the great processions was pitiful; so much had been destroyed. But they went back to their own camps refreshed and restored, remembering and mourning the many who had died or surrendered in the single year since their great victory over the Blue Coats at the Little Big Horn battle.

Brings Horses Woman kept her vow to do little good things, since she could not hope to do big ones, as her mother, Whirlwind, had. In her brother's lodge, the burns of his wife Young Bird had healed, leaving one side of her face hideous. That side of her scalp had been burned so that her hair did not grow there again. She hid her face with her shawl all the time outside the lodge, ashamed to be seen.

After much thought and pity, Brings Horses made her a present, a bonnet of buckskin. Lakota women did not wear hats but Brings Horses had seen sunbonnets on the wagon-train women who went by Fort Laramie. What she made did not shade the face, like those. It was more like a deep cap, and at each side she sewed bluebird wings that covered the cheeks and looked very pretty. Young Bird had only one braid of hair now, but Brings

Horses figured out how to conceal that one-sidedness. She made a matching braid with black hair from a horse's tail and wound it with otter skin for a braid wrapping. She sewed it in the proper place on the bonnet.

Then she went to visit Young Bird with the things hidden under her blanket. "Close your eyes, I want to give you something," she said. "Close them tight!"

She put the cap on her sister-in-law with its one wrapped braid; then she wrapped the other braid with otter skin to match. Young Bird whimpered a little: "I am ugly. Nothing is any use to hide the scars."

"You are brave; everybody knows it, but you forget that warriors have scars." Brings Horses held up a small mirror. "Now look! You are pretty. You are a warrior with feathers!"

Young Bird looked and stared and cried out with pleasure. She always wore the bonnet after that, or another like it, and held her head high and was proud.

3

Refugees

Slowly the Lakotas who had moved to the Grand-mother's Land rebuilt their lives. The men hunted hard, the women worked tirelessly so there would be furs and hides to trade for the lost things that needed to be replaced. The young men were restless, because without war, how could they win honor? Sometimes, secretly, a few crossed the line, unseen by the Grand-mother's police, who could not be everywhere. The young men took horses now and then from the Wasi-chu settlements in Montana Territory without being caught, but there was no great glory in it, because they dared not boast.

And secretly, singly or in pairs, riders came with news from the Great Sioux Reservation in Dakota Territory to tell how badly the people were being treated there, how poor and ragged and hungry they were.

No matter how hard the men hunted in Canada, there was barely enough to eat, and this was true also of the Grandmother's own Indians, those who had always been there. Where were the great endless herds of buffalo that

27

had always roamed the prairies without regard to the Medicine Line?

Blue Rock Woman said one day, sighing, "I have nothing to do. The men can't make meat when there is nothing to kill. And we are surrounded by enemies. The Grandmother's Indians hate us."

Brings Horses answered, "But now we have Sitting Bull with us, and his medicine is powerful. Everything is going to be all right."

Elk Rising's brother, still limping from his wound, was not so sure. "Something is keeping the buffalo away. The Grandmother's Indians have not enough meat either."

Sitting Bull often had meetings with the Red Coats' chief, Major Walsh. A tough man but honest, he never lied. He kept urging Sitting Bull to take his people back to the Grandfather's land, to the reservation that was promised there.

"You will receive rations there when there are no buffalo," he promised, "and land of your own."

Officials from the United States kept trying to persuade the Lakotas to return. Sitting Bull sneered at them. But with the red-coated Major Walsh he was friends.

That was a terrible summer, 1877, for another tribe of Indians, the Nez Percés, who had lived long in the northeast corner of Oregon. Their chief was called Joseph, after his father. They raised cattle and fine spotted horses. The Wasichu settlers wanted their land, so the soldiers said they must move to a reservation. They tried to move, although their hearts were on the ground, but they could not round up their stock in a hurry because their cows were calving. A soldier chief with one arm, General Oliver Howard, sent soldiers to make them move, and settlers stole some of the Indians' good horses and cattle.

So there was a battle, and other Nez Percés flocked to join Chief Joseph's band. Their chiefs decided to flee eastward, over the Rocky Mountains—they knew the prairie country, because they sometimes hunted buffalo there.

They were resting in a camp in the Big Hole Valley when other soldiers, led by a soldier chief named John Gibbon, attacked them at dawn one day in August. In the Battle of the Big Hole, the soldiers did great butchery.

The survivors headed south and east through Yellowstone Park, intending to seek help from the Crows. But the Crows refused; they were allies of the white men and would not fight them.

News of some of these battles and of the long, hard wandering of the Nez Percés reached the Lakotas in Canada by moccasin telegraph. There was much talk in the Lakota camps. The restless young men wanted to go south and help, but the chiefs reminded them with forceful oratory that this would endanger *all* the Lakotas. They had promised to stay north of the Medicine Line, and mostly they did.

The Lakotas were not surprised, of course, to learn that the Crows had refused to help other Indians. In their opinion, the Crows were utterly worthless people and always had been. Fire arrows shot from the bows of Crow scouts for the soldiers had burned Lakota lodges on the way north.

In September the desperate Nez Percés, heading north across Montana, sent one of their fighting chiefs, White Bird, to see Sitting Bull. White Bird crossed the Medicine Line without being seen and found Sitting Bull. They talked a little, and Sitting Bull called a council. White Bird pleaded for help from the Lakotas.

With a stick he drew in the dirt a picture of the route his people had taken, the mountains they had crossed, the places where they had fought the Blue Coats. All this long way they had lived off the country, fought the white soldiers, mourned their dead, protected their women and children and wounded. They were ragged and hungry and weak.

"We need brave young men, strong fighting men," White Bird pleaded, "to help us the rest of the way."

The chiefs were stirred. How they wanted to unleash their young men—and go with them! But Sitting Bull could not let them, although his heart was on the ground.

"We have promised to stay in Canada," he said. "The woman chief across the water does not want us here, and if we break our promise her red-coat policemen will let the Grandfather's Blue Coats kill us. The Red Coats said so, and they always do what they promise."

So White Bird rode back sadly to his suffering people and gave Chief Joseph the bad news. The Nez Percés kept moving north. They camped at last on the northern edge of the Bear Paw Mountains, thinking they had reached Canada and safety. They were exhausted.

But they were thirty miles south of the Medicine Line. General Miles, Bear Coat, attacked them with six hundred soldiers. On the fourth day of the fighting, October 5, the one-armed Howard came with more soldiers. And Chief Joseph surrendered, never to be free again.

He made a solemn promise from a breaking heart:

"From where the sun now stands, I will fight no more forever."

Major Walsh, White Forehead, had kept urging Sitting Bull to take his people back to the United States. The stubborn Old Man Chief kept refusing, but they remained friends. Then a commission of very important Americans, sent by their government, asked permission to come into Canada to talk to the chief. Sitting Bull didn't want to see them or listen to them, but Walsh managed to persuade him. The council would be held at Fort Walsh.

They were just about ready to set out when two messengers arrived—one happened to be Sitting Bull's faithful hero-worshiper, young Standing Tree, who seemed to be everywhere—with news:

"The Nez Percés surrendered, but some got away in the dark. They are coming now—White Bird and maybe two hundred people, seeking refuge. They are wounded and starving."

Sitting Bull was furious. "We will care for them—and I will not go to meet those Americans at Fort Walsh. Go tell the people!"

His scouts galloped off to alert the nearest camps. The women hastened to make their lodges ready for these sufferers. The Nez Percés came, wounded and wailing, hungry and grieving, carrying small children who had an arm or a leg broken by a Wasichu bullet. Walsh himself saw a woman ride across the line with her baby on her back in her shawl, although she had been shot in the breast so the bullet came out her back. There were almost one hundred men, wounded and bloodstained, about fifty exhausted women, and the same number of

31

children. With them they brought three hundred horses.

Now the Lakotas were furious indeed, even while they scurried to make places to comfort and care for the refugee Nez Percés. Only a few days before, angry messengers had come with news from the Oglalas who had surrendered the previous spring. Their great chief Crazy Horse was dead! He had been stabbed by a blue-coat soldier in the army's guardhouse.

They put aside their grief and anger, for this was the time for compassion. Brings Horses welcomed two of the strangers, a boy of four winters with a bullet hole in his leg and a bone broken there, and a young woman who talked interminably in a frantic way and did not know where she was or, Brings Horses thought, even who she was.

Gently, gently, the women in the lodge cared for the little boy. One held him down while another set his broken bone and tied a splint on it. He screamed steadily, and Brings Horses kept saying, "There, there, little warrior." They did not know his language, but he understood the tone of her voice.

"If nobody claims him," Brings Horses announced, "this will be my little boy, whom the Great Mystery gave me in place of the one who sleeps in a tree with his grandmother back there. And he will bear the same name she gave my boy."

Sitting Bull himself rode with White Bird through the camp to see where the refugees were staying and what their condition was. Always, at a polite distance behind them, rode Standing Tree, hoping to be sent on an errand or asked to do something useful. He never intruded. He was just always there.

When they came to his own home, the lodge of Elk Rising, the two chiefs dismounted. Standing Tree shouted in Lakota to the women inside, "The great chiefs are here! Let them in." Sitting Bull almost smiled; he was a grim, unsmiling man.

Brings Horses came to the door and invited them to come in. Blue Rock hastened to invite Sitting Bull to sit in the place of honor, because the lodge master was not at home, and she spread a good robe for White Bird.

The two chiefs talked briefly in sign language; they spoke with some pauses, because the language was not exactly the same for tribes that had lived so far apart. Sitting Bull translated into Lakota for the women:

"The Nez Percé child is an orphan. Both parents were killed. He has no relatives living."

Brings Horses snatched up the little boy and cuddled him, asking eagerly, "Then can we have him? My baby died when we were running from the soldiers. My mother gave him a name, her name, a great name that Crazy Horse himself gave her for her bravery. It was Saved Her Cub. I would call this child by that name."

Sitting Bull signed at some length to the Nez Percé leader and answered, "White Bird says you can have him. You are a good woman."

The Nez Percé woman who usually talked too much had been looking vacantly into space. Now she recognized White Bird and began her repetitious talking again. White Bird spoke sharply to her in their own language, but she stopped talking for only a moment.

He explained through Sitting Bull, "She lost everyone at the Big Hole and was hurt in the head. She keeps talking about that battle."

Sitting Bull told the women, "She is *wakan,* holy."

Even her own people, the Nez Percés, were tired of hearing her, White Bird explained. Nobody could stand it forever. But she could work if someone would look after her—and pretend to listen sometimes.

Sitting Bull, who had medicine powers himself, warned that there was no medicine to cure that madness, but patience and kindness would ease her misery a little.

Brings Horses remembered: I cannot do great things like my mother, but I can do little things. Listening to the woman's wearisome chatter, she remembered also that the other occupants of the lodge could not endure it forever.

She said timidly, "We can make her a small lodge of her own, and sometimes I will listen."

Sitting Bull explained to White Bird and translated his reply: "You are a good woman."

They walked out and mounted their horses.

Brings Horses resolved: I will teach her to whisper, so she will not bother other people. And sometimes, if she cries, I will cry with her.

Thus she made life bearable for the family in the lodge and for the pitiful Nez Percé whom they called Wakan Woman.

For a long time official visitors had been trying to persuade Sitting Bull to return to the United States. Because he was the head chief of thousands of desperate Indians, the Canadian government considered him dangerous. He had fooled and eluded the Blue Coats, so the United States wanted him on a reservation where he could be closely guarded. The Americans feared that he would sweep down and kill their people. Canada belonged to Grandmother England; the Queen's government far away wanted him to leave her territory north of the Medicine Line. If he and the angry people whom he led crossed the line to attack in the United States, there could be war between those nations.

But Sitting Bull was as stubborn a man as ever was born. Major Walsh did much talking, much persuading, before he convinced the Old Man Chief of all the Lakotas that he should meet with a commission of important men from the Grandfather in Washington. They met in October, in a big room at Fort Walsh. Sitting Bull had with him twenty-four other chiefs. He entered with immense dignity, shook hands with the Canadians, and totally ignored the Americans. He sat down with his back to the visitors.

After all the chiefs had sat down, a lone woman entered, the wife of Bear That Scatters. It was unheard of that a woman should attend a high-level council, but Sitting Bull had planned this. She was there to deliver an insult to the Americans.

General Alfred Terry spoke eloquently, making big promises. He was a tall man, six feet six, taller even than the Lakotas.

He promised that if they came back, they would not be punished, they would have land for farming, they would receive food and clothing. But they could not come ready to make war. They would have to give up their guns and ammunition and all their horses except those needed for peaceful purposes.

Sitting Bull spoke at length. What he meant was "You treated us badly and we don't want to hear any more of your nonsense."

Other chiefs spoke, saying about the same thing.

Then the lone woman, whose very presence was an insult, stood up and spoke. An interpreter translated:

"You kept us running all the time so I never had time to—" He stopped, looking puzzled. "She say she will stay here because down south you never gave her time to—" He stopped again, searching for a polite English word. He asked another interpreter, who replied with a grin. Then he finished: "You never gave her time to breed."

The woman walked out, leaving the Wasichus embarrassed, exactly as had been planned.

The big council was, from the point of view of everyone who wanted to get the Lakotas out of Canada, a dismal failure. White people on both sides of the Medicine Line shuddered. With a leader like Sitting Bull at the head of all those angry Indians, there could be bloody war.

Major Walsh's superior, Colonel James McLeod, warned the chiefs at the meeting, "Now you can never go back with guns or ammunition. If you or your young men ever cross the line with arms in your hands, then we become your enemies as the Americans are. The buffalo will not last very much longer."

4

Where Is the Future?

Buffalo hunting was only fairly good in 1878, the second year the people of Sitting Bull lived in Canada. Meat and robes were sufficient but not plentiful. The buffalo herds that came north were small, and too many Indians hunted them. The Queen's Indians, who had always lived there, were sullen toward the newcomers.

One of the hardest things to get used to was the Queen's rule against warfare. In Morning Rider's lodge, young Kills Grizzly had gained his medicine, his protective power, just at the time of the big fight at the Little Big Horn; he was ready to be a warrior, but there could be no war now, and no horse stealing, so how could he gain honors? Of course he *had* killed the grizzly bear, also a blue-coat soldier when the camp was attacked on the way to Canada. He was a proven fighter, and could wear an eagle feather in his hair. But what future was there for him?

A young man of the Lakotas could not rest forever on youthful proof of valor. One brave deed must follow another. Now the whole system was ruined.

Angry, a year younger, went out to lament for a medicine helper in the spring of 1878 and was successful. His medicine was the Hawk, and his manhood name was Hawk Child, after a distant ancestor. He was brave and ambitious—but how could he prove it? He had not counted coup—touched an enemy—in the battle on the way to Canada; he had protected women and children, as he was ordered to do. He could not wear an eagle feather.

Hawk Child listened with respect to the coup stories related by youths only a year or two older than himself, and he took pride in his half-brother's qualifications to boast in the company of warriors, but his envy was bitter. One Hunkpapa who had lived only fourteen winters before the great, victorious battle on the Little Big Horn gloried in this tale:

"I had no gun, but I shot a soldier on horseback from the side with an arrow. It went under his ribs from one side to the other and stuck out on both sides. The soldier screamed and hung onto his saddle horn and swayed. I rode up beside him and hit him across the back of the neck with my heavy bow. He fell off and I jumped off my horse and beat him to death with my bow, I was so furious because the soldiers had our women and children so frightened and out of breath on the other side of the river. Those Wasichus wanted it, and they came to get it, and we gave it to them!"

The young men and boys who were listening roared approval, remembering that great day. The youth added, grinning, "A little boy asked me to scalp a soldier for him and took the scalp to his mother. I did, and then I rode home, leading a good American horse, to get something to eat. Anyway, I was tired of the smell of blood."

Envious Hawk Child—Angry—thought that only a real warrior would dare to admit that.

Elk Rising had a big family. Now there were Saved Her Cub, the Nez Percé orphan, and Wakan Woman, who talked all the time. She had a small lodge of her own but was a member of the family. When her constant, unintelligible chatter made the others cross, someone took her to her little lodge, sometimes with a small child to love and cuddle. These refugees were in addition to the family Elk Rising already had.

He sometimes said, "I don't know whether Standing Tree lives with us or not. He is seldom here. He keeps his clothes here and sleeps here sometimes or comes to eat, but he is always somewhere near Sitting Bull. He worships the chief. Well, Sitting Bull is a great man. I hope Standing Tree does not get in the way."

White Mountain smiled. "If he did, the chief would send him off fast enough. Maybe he's learning something. Maybe he's useful."

Sitting Bull had organized a special group of one hundred strong, alert Hunkpapa warriors soon after the Little Big Horn fight, a kind of police force accountable to him alone, different from the warrior societies. They were known as "Sitting Bull's Soldiers." They gloried in the honor of belonging to him.

Elk Rising said, "Do you think Standing Tree hopes to be chosen for one of Sitting Bull's Soldiers? They are all older than he is, with lots of war honors."

White Mountain didn't think so. "He is a hero worshiper, and Sitting Bull is his hero. That is not a bad thing. He only wants to serve him. He runs errands like a little boy. But when we hunt buffalo, he is with us, and his meat is for us and Morning Rider's family." Suddenly bitter, White Mountain burst out, "I am no good, Brother. My hip is always bad; I am not agile. I limp."

Elk Rising reminded him, "Sitting Bull limps, too, ever since he was a young man and was wounded in the foot by an arrow."

That comforted White Mountain a little.

And so life went on; they were safe from the blue-coat soldiers, but they could not live as in the old days, seeking honor in the old ways. Frustration boiled in the young men, and it was hard for Sitting Bull to keep them to the promises he had made to White Forehead, Major Walsh. When they broke the Queen's laws, the chief himself punished them harshly. They endured the punishment and did not resent it.

There was little meat to store for winter, there were few robes to take to the traders, but next year—ah, surely next year would be better. The buffalo had always been. Would they not always graze their way north in the spring?

But they did not. Almost none came to the Grandmother's land in the spring of 1879. Was the Great Mystery angry? The Queen's Indians blamed the newcomers. The Lakotas blamed the Queen's Indians. And there were those who blamed the United States Army.

Because all along the border, for uncounted miles, the dry wild grass had been burned the previous fall. Many fires had been set purposely. The Queen's Red Coats rode far, examining the spring grass—bright green but thin, in scanty clumps. Fire had not killed the grass roots, but the buffalo, moving north, had found poor grazing and had turned aside. They had not crossed into Canada where the hungry Indians waited.

So great was the anger about that grass-burning, so black was the suspicion among the tribes, that the Bloods and the Piegans almost went to war against the Lakotas. But Major Walsh upheld the Queen's law in the case of the Queen's Indians, too. He would not let them fight. The Blackfeet, related to these other tribes, did ride south to where the buffalo were, in the United States.

Scouts reported to Sitting Bull: "The Blackfeet went south to the buffalo. We saw them cross. We should go down there, too."

The chief seldom showed surprise and did not show it now. He thought for a moment. "The Blackfeet are the Queen's Indians. She has not made any rule saying that they cannot cross the Medicine Line and come back again. This was their home all the time. But we cannot go—or if we do, we cannot come back here. We promised the Major."

Some of his special soldiers muttered. Their families were hungry, and their great leader knew it. But he spoke truly about the promise. He was caught in a trap. There was no use arguing. Eloquence in oratory meant nothing to the wolf of hunger; it had no ears.

The Lakotas had a hope: perhaps this time Sitting Bull himself would close his ears and his eyes. Very quietly, a few men talked about this. Secretly and singly they visited the lodges of the very best hunters in the big camp and summoned them to private councils.

Elk Rising was one of those summoned. He was known as a great hunter. A minor chief, who would lead the expedition, explained the plan: "We will have fifty good hunters with their buffalo horses, and plenty more horses for packing. We will take skilled women to do the skinning and butchering and keep the camp. We are not going to war. We are going to bring back meat!"

They moved out quietly, almost four hundred people and many horses. Sitting Bull closed his eyes and ears.

Elk Rising and his wife Brings Horses were among them. The hunters used strong bows and plenty of arrows, partly because an arrow flies in silence and partly because they had little ammunition for their guns. Ammunition had to come from the traders, and they had nothing to buy it with.

They rode south, and the buffalo were there. The men rode like the wind and shot straight. The women skinned and butchered the great shaggy carcasses. There was much meat and much joy.

They were almost ready to start back when their old enemy Bear Coat, Colonel Miles, attacked them. His Indian scouts had reported the hunt. He came upon the hunters and their women suddenly and attacked.

The Lakotas were not ready for war, but the men fought back hard while the women fled, taking the meat-laden horses as fast as they could go. The Lakota hunters retreated north, fighting as they went, using bows and arrows. Two *akícitas* rode north for help with their horses at a dead run.

Brings Horses, whipping her saddle horse and hurrying along three meat-loaded packhorses with her whip as she dashed back and forth, was afraid—but she had been afraid before. Other women, too, kept their heads and hurried their horses, never looking back, trying not to hear the gunfire of the blue-coat soldiers. This was a time to act, not to worry or to cry, a time for women to trust their men, who fought with silent, fast-flying arrows, protecting them. It was a time for the men to trust their women to take home all the meat they could.

One packhorse went down. Brings Horses left it, whipping those she had left. The women did not scream; they saved their breath, riding north. There was plenty of noise behind them from the soldiers' guns and the warriors' brave-up shouts. She hoped they had plenty of arrows. Every man had pulled his arrows out of the beasts he shot and picked up any he found loose.

Brings Horses heard a woman up ahead yell, "The stone piles! And someone is coming from there!"

Just then Brings Horses felt a hard blow on her left arm and saw her own blood flowing from the wound. All of them were bloody anyway from the butchering.

"So that is what a bullet feels like," she thought, and kept on whipping her horses, kept on riding. The wound did not hurt yet.

Sitting Bull, who had pretended to close his eyes and ears, had moved down close to the border with some of his people. Now, rules or no rules, he led his fighting men across the line to pass the frantic women and go on to help the men against the Wasichus. But the shooting had stopped now. The Blue Coats did not come any closer. They did not fire across the sacred Medicine Line.

Perhaps there were too many angry Indians swarming down upon their relatively small force.

Brings Horses felt strangely weak and dizzy after she pulled up her sweating horse. A strong warrior, seeing her sway in the saddle, helped her to the ground, and she laughed.

"I have not needed help in dismounting from a horse

43

since I was four winters old," she said. "Is Elk Rising safe?" Then the world went away. She fainted.

He was safe, not hurt. Some men were wounded, none killed. They had made meat, to be divided among all the people. When the world came back, someone gave Brings Horses water to drink and bound up her wounded arm with a piece of trader's cloth. But when they started to lift her onto a pony drag, she was angry.

"I will walk to our lodge," she announced. "The bullet only struck my arm. I do not walk with my arms!"

Her husband answered firmly, "You will go on the pony drag because I say so," and she gave in meekly. It was pleasant to be loved and cared for. She felt like a young bride again, all those years ago before she had responsibilities.

"Maybe you should have a new name," he said. "Shall we call you Brings Much Meat?"

"I will not answer to it," she replied, smiling. "All I did was help carry the meat."

That was only a little thing that I did, she told herself; no more than the other women did. But my mother, Whirlwind, would be glad.

Brings Horses was embarrassed about being unable to help cut up the meat and apportion it to those who had none. Her arm was swollen and hot, and it hurt a great deal. She said, apologizing, "When the hunters who were really hurt do not need the medicine priests any more, maybe you could take me to one of them."

"One is coming to you now," Elk Rising told her.

"Wolf Chief is coming. No, no, lie still. You do not need to do anything."

Wolf Chief came, with his tools and bags of herbs, dried blood still on his hands. Blue Rock Woman let him in and hovered, ready to do anything she could to help. She had a kettle of hot water ready, and a bowl and a kettle of cold water.

Wolf Chief nodded approval. "I want warm water in the bowl," he said, "and a small piece of soft buckskin." Chanting prayers and spells, he washed the dried blood gently from around the wound so he could get a better look at it.

"The bone is not broken," he said, "but the bullet is still in there. So I will take it out."

Chanting, he laid some herbs on the fire to make a fragrant, sacred smoke. He took a pinch of some other herb that was ground to a powder and laid it on Brings Horses' tongue. "Chew that and swallow it," he ordered.

He laid out his tools: a knife, honed to thinness, and a sharp awl of the kind women used for piercing tiny holes in buckskin for fine embroidery with beads or porcupine quills.

He looked at Brings Horses' husband and said, "You can hold her down to keep her arm steady if she struggles against the pain."

Elk Rising sounded shocked as he replied, "My wife will not struggle against the pain. She is a true Lakota! But I will steady her arm for you."

She did not struggle or cry out while Wolf Chief cut and probed and took the bullet out, because her man loved her and she was the daughter of Whirlwind.

When the priest said, "There, it is finished," she permitted herself to sigh.

"I will wear the bullet on a necklace," she announced.

Later, Sitting Bull had to face Major Walsh, who reminded him, "You broke your promise. You broke the Queen's law!"

The chief knew when to act humble, when to explain and placate. "I could not control my hunters," he admitted. "Our women and children were hungry. We went without permission. Punish us however the Queen's law requires."

Major Walsh could understand thoroughly what had happened. There had already been punishment—there were wounded, and some horses and meat had been lost. He held a formal meeting with Colonel Miles and, in spite of his embarrassment at being unable to control his Indians, explained and apologized, so they parted friends, respecting each other.

Sitting Bull was now leader of more than a thousand warriors, all well mounted, all burning with resentment at the Wasichus south of the border. They were a menace to both Canada and the United States. Walsh called a big council and talked to all of them. As he had done many times before, he said, "If you hunt south of the stone piles, you cannot come back. I will turn the Americans loose on you."

He reminded them again, "You are not the Queen's Indians. You should go to your reservation in the United States, and that government will see that you have food."

A priest from Dakota, Father Marty, had come to tell them this before; now he came again and repeated it.

The Lakotas did not trust him. He spoke for the forked-tongue men. They trusted only Sitting Bull and Walsh. But the future was so bleak that some of them were willing to listen and think about it. Some of the Queen's Indians, hungry because the buffalo were so scarce, were receiving rations from the Queen's government, but there would never be any for the Lakotas.

That summer, at the usual time, they held the Sun-gazing Dance in the old, reverent way and prayed with unusual fervor to the Great Mystery for a message of deliverance. But the only message the desperate vision-seekers had was one of despair: You can't go on living this way.

An old medicine priest made up a sad song and his reedy voice could often be heard singing it to the music of his small drum:

> "Is a voice promising something?
> Does the Great Mystery speak to us?
> It says, 'We have forsaken you.'
> It says, 'We have thrown you away.' "

PART II

THE BITTER
TASTE OF DEFEAT

1880

5

Families Divided

The next winter was gaunt. Any small animal was food, and any root that filled one's stomach without making the stomach sick. Even brave warriors helped the desperate women search for such tiny, contemptible game as field mice in their burrows. Starvation moved among the people like a snake, silent and slow.

Walsh's men felt such pity for the hunger around them that there was no longer so much as a crust wasted from their own rations. They did not put out garbage any more. They saved clean scraps and sometimes did not themselves eat as much of the Queen's rations as they would have liked, but kept everything possible for the stew kettles in the lodges.

And still, the women used their knives on carcasses of horses a long time dead, and many people became sick because of this.

Some of the people, already weak from hunger, were so sick from eating the bad meat that they died. Blue Rock Woman, that sad wife of Elk Rising, had grieved ever since the death of her little boy, Beaver. Now her spirit left her wasted body and set forth to be reunited with his spirit in the Land of Many Lodges.

Brings Horses Woman said, with tears on her cheeks, "I think she was glad to go."

Sitting Bull was as thin as the rest of them, but more stubborn than most. "I will never shake hands with an American," he repeated. Then, sadly, "But those of the people who wish to go back may do so. Maybe the Americans do not all lie. Maybe there is food down there."

In March of 1880 many Lakotas had already gone south, and now thirty more families rode sadly away. Major Walsh helped them by giving their head men letters to carry, requesting agents and army officers to protect them on their way to the agencies on the reservation.

Chiefs Broadtail and Little Knife led one hundred more lodges to Poplar Creek in Montana and received rations at once. In April, Iron Dog, Waterspout, Hairy Chin, and Killed the White Man set out for the agencies at Spotted Tail and Red Cloud. Major Walsh reported to his superiors that ten more chiefs with 250 families had gone south.

Even Morning Rider and his family left—they were Oglalas and never so close to Sitting Bull as Elk Rising, who was a Hunkpapa. Brings Horses said good-bye tearfully to her brother and his family. She was a Hunkpapa by marriage, and she never questioned the decision of her man to stay.

Those who were parting embraced, and the women cried. Even Wakan Woman, the mad Nez Percé, wept when she parted from the Oglala family, although surely she did not know who they were or why there was sadness.

Morning Rider and Elk Rising smoked together one

last time and talked about where those surrendering might be sent by the Wasichu Blue Coats south of the Medicine Line. They hoped for better things at whatever agency the surrendered hostiles might be ordered to, but what they really expected they did not tell each other. The Grandfather in Washington had promised much, and every time they could remember, he had lied. But maybe there would be more food down there. There could hardly be less than they had now.

And so Brings Horses and her husband and their household watched with breaking hearts as the Oglalas rode off: Morning Rider, his wife Young Bird (wearing her buckskin bonnet with bluebird feathers at the sides), his other wife Brown Leaf Woman, and the children—Hawk Child and Kills Grizzly, old enough to be warriors now, and Reaches Far Girl, and the little boy with the honorable name, She Throws Him.

Sitting Bull had said, "I will be the last to go. The Americans will kill me, I think. I have never been afraid to fight or die, but let it be for a worthwhile cause, not shamefully stabbed in a jail like Crazy Horse."

In summer, Walsh was transferred by order of his superiors. He could not help the Lakotas any more. Besides, he was sick, had been sick a long time.

Their parting was not a ceremony, as many of their meetings had been. There was no gathering of chiefs and warriors, no grim guardianship by Sitting Bull's chosen "soldiers." Almost all of these had gone now, taking their families to surrender. But Standing Tree was there, alert, quiet, part of the scenery. He saw the parting. The chief wore his fine warbonnet of nodding eagle plumes. He wore it seldom.

Walsh made a promise: "Old friend, I will do what I

can for you. I am going farther south than your people have gone, to some hot springs, for my health. I am going to Washington where the President is. I will try to see him, try to tell him you are not to blame for everything bad that ever happened. I will try to do that, old friend. But I am not a high chief of the Queen. In the United States I am no chief at all. Still, I will do everything I can for you."

Sitting Bull replied, "I am through fighting." He took off his fine warbonnet and held it out. "I want you to have this, friend."

When Standing Tree related that story at home, he grieved, "I think they took White Forehead away because he helped us all he could. Nobody will help us any more.

"And now the chief has something more to worry about. His oldest daughter, of seventeen winters, ran away with a young man and went south in the last bunch of people who left. The chief does not say anything, but he grieves about her."

Sitting Bull now had two wives, who were sisters, three sons, and one daughter remaining. The youngest family members were twin boys of four winters. His other son, Crowfoot, was seven.

Sitting Bull lost another old friend, Chief Gall, who had fought well in many battles including the Little Big Horn. Now Gall turned against him and started south with half the Lakotas who remained in the Grandmother's country.

In the middle of December, Sitting Bull himself gave up. With the pitifully few of his people who were left, he headed southward.

But a scout reached him with news that Gall and his people were in trouble. Gall had surrendered south of the border but he could not get his followers to Fort Buford by the date the army officers set, January 2, 1881. They were too hungry and weak; they could not move so fast. The officers had ordered the soldiers to attack Gall's people.

When Sitting Bull learned of that cruelty, he and his little band turned back into Canada. He could not find Walsh. His people were starving on roots and field mice. He found a Catholic priest hauling some supplies to his mission and traded the blanket off his own back for a sack of flour. There had been a time when the Lakotas threw flour away, not knowing what to do with it, but now the women had learned to make a kind of bread that they fried over the fire.

Standing Tree rode always now near Sitting Bull when the people moved, but he slept in his own place in the lodge of Elk Rising, and he brought news and gossip. For a long time everyone had known that the head chief worried about his missing daughter. Now Standing Tree could tell those in his own lodge, "The chief had news from a scout that his daughter is a captive at Fort Yates and the soldiers keep her in chains there. She surrendered with her man at Fort Buford."

The people hoped it was not true. Sitting Bull had enough to worry about. But they trusted him. They had nobody else to lead them now.

And the chief had nobody to help him with supplies —except one good man. His name was Jean Louis Legare, and he was an honest trader with whom they had done business when they had robes to trade. He was not only honest, he was kind. He had watched their sufferings. He undertook to help them get to the United States while they had strength enough to move.

The Canadian government was glad to have him do it.

Legare supplied creaking, two-wheeled wagons heaped with supplies to feed Sitting Bull's remaining followers. He invested a great sum of his own money in this, expecting one government or the other to pay him back. (But they never did.)

They arrived on July 19, 1881, at Fort Buford, where the Yellowstone River flows into the Missouri, some seventy miles south of the border. Army troops were lined up and waiting.

The Wasichu officers gave orders, and officious interpreters shouted them to the defeated people in Lakota:

"Men line up over here. Women and children stay back. Hurry up!"

The people obeyed, but not very fast. They were weak from hunger, although Legare had fed them all the rations he carried in his wagons.

"Every man who has a gun, give it to the soldiers!" They handed over their guns, one by one. The soldiers also took their ammunition, if they had any left. Soldiers carried these things away.

"Every man throw down his bow!" There was a murmur among the people. Some bows were too sacred to throw down. The captives carefully laid them down on a blanket that had been spread. Now indeed they were helpless before their conquerors.

"You will get the bows back, maybe, so you can hunt." There were sighs of relief among the people.

They did not have to give up their knives; without a knife, one could not cut meat to eat.

"All but the chiefs and head men must give up their horses. They can keep only one apiece."

Soldiers went out to the pony herd and chased the

Indian boys back to join their families. There was some delay while Sitting Bull and other leaders chose the one horse each would keep.

The women and children huddled together, watching, hardly breathing. Red Pipe Girl said to her mother, "Why do you keep rubbing the bullet scar on your arm with your other hand? Is there medicine power in it?"

Brings Horses was startled. "I didn't know I was doing that." She thought for a moment. "Maybe there is power in it to make me brave. It makes me remember about helping your father bring home meat, and about being struck by a bullet." She smiled dreamily, in spite of the terror around them and the fear of what might come. "It helps me remember that he said he was proud of me because I was brave."

She stooped and hugged her little girl. "You must remember all we have told you about your grandmother Whirlwind. She was very brave, a warrior woman in courage although she never fought in battle as men do. I can't do great things as she did. But I do little things, remembering her.

"Now stand straight, and so will I. Your father stands straight, see? Because we are still Lakotas."

When the conquerors got around to it, they issued rations so the defeated, famished people of Sitting Bull could eat. He went around the camp to make sure everyone had something before he sat down for his own food. That was the right way for a great chief to act.

One good thing happened at Fort Buford. Sitting Bull learned from an officer that his runaway daughter was not a prisoner in chains. She was well and living at one of the agencies.

CANADA
(Grandmother's Land)

Milk River

Bear Paw
Mountains

Missouri River

Fort Buford

MONTANA

NORTH DAKOTA

Mandan

Heart River

Yellowstone River

Fort Yates — Standing Rock Agency

Custer's
Last Stand

Sitting Bull's Encampment ×

General Crook &
Crazy Horse
Fight

Grand River

Little Big Horn R.

Powder River

SOUTH DAKOTA

Missouri River

Big Horn River

WYOMING

Bad Lands

White River

Rosebud
Landing

Rosebud   Agency

Pine Ridge Agency   Wounded Knee

Fort Randall

Fort Robinson

Red Cloud Agency

Niobrara

River

Fort Laramie

North

Platte

River

NEBRASKA

COLORADO

Lodgepole Cr.

Platte

River

KANSAS

0   25   50   100
MILES
Map by Salem Tamer

Forts 〜 ~ Agencies

6

━━━━━━━━━━━━━━━

The Prison

The people were kept at Fort Buford for days, with nobody telling them what was going to happen next. Then they were herded onto a big fireboat to travel down the Missouri River. This thoroughly frightened the women (most of whom did not admit it as long as their men were near them) and caused many of the children to scream in fear. Some of the adults had seen fireboats before but few had ever been close to one. The Wasichus called them steamboats. They were floating monsters that ate wood and belched smoke. Usually they did not travel at night for fear of running aground in the hazardous river.

The small children were so frightened by all the strangeness that they cried and had to be soothed with stories. Red Pipe Girl was nine and had already endured through many fears and dangers, but she clung close to her mother, Brings Horses Woman. The adopted Nez Percé boy, called Saved Her Cub, was about the same age, and he had been through terrors, too. But as a man-to-be, he considered it beneath him to show fear.

He tried to stay close to his adopted father, Elk Rising, and his adopted brother, Stormy, who was twelve.

Red Pipe Girl kept demanding, "Where are we going and what will they do to us?"

Brings Horses told her, "It is a surprise. Some nice place, with plenty to eat."

The little girl was really afraid then. "The Land of Many Lodges!" she burst out. "They are going to kill us and we will go there and be happy."

"Sometime we all will go there," her mother promised, "but not yet. This is another place." She was not at all sure of that.

There were rumors among the people, passed on from interpreters who mingled with the soldiers; the soldiers didn't really know either. The fireboat snorted and howled its way down the Missouri.

One thing the captives knew: most of the Hunkpapa Lakotas who had surrendered before them were now at an agency called Standing Rock, and the soldiers' place there was called Fort Yates. So Standing Rock was probably where Sitting Bull's people would be told to live.

They were all tired of the fireboat. Rations had run very low, so they were hungry again. Before they reached Fort Yates, almost three hundred miles downriver from Fort Buford where they had surrendered, the fireboat pulled in for a landing at Mandan and they were marched ashore, where they were held in a group by a hollow-square formation of armed soldiers.

Some officers came and hunted out Sitting Bull and a few other head men, explaining to them through interpreters what was going to happen: these few men would be taken to the town by carriage for a meal and to have a photograph made. Women and children began to wail in sorrow, assuming the men were to be killed. Sitting Bull stood up in the carriage, seeming unafraid, and calmed his people.

Then the soldiers issued enough rations for two days —but the women cooked everything right away over fires they built there on shore, and all the food was eaten in three hours.

After Sitting Bull and the other head men were brought back, the people were herded onto the fireboat again, and it steamed on down the river sixty miles more toward Standing Rock and Fort Yates.

Families huddled together as the fireboat slowed at Fort Yates. People murmured, "Now we will see our friends and relatives again, and find out how the Wasi-chus want us to live." Some of the children were crying with the doleful wail of little ones who have been hungry for so long that they can hardly remember feeling good.

By the rail, with other people crowding, stood Elk Rising, with one hand on the shoulder of his son Stormy and one on the Nez Percé boy. Brings Horses Woman held the hand of little Red Pipe Girl and firmly grasped the quivering arm of Wakan Woman, who was silent for once.

On the shore hundreds of Indians stood, waving and shouting greetings, particularly to Sitting Bull, who stood with his family around him, staring at the shore. On the fireboat, some of the people began to sing. Chief Gall was there on shore; a chief named Running Ante-lope did not even wait for the landing stage to swing into place but leaped on board and embraced Sitting Bull, whose tears ran down his cheeks.

The newcomers were made to camp by themselves on a river bench, apart from their friends. Soldiers swung their rifles and kept them in order. Their lodges and clothing were ragged, they were hungry, unarmed and almost naked—but now they could settle down. Or could they?

No. A military order came: Sitting Bull and his immediate followers, those who had remained hostile to the end, must be punished.

An interpreter said, "You will ride on the fireboat some more to a place called Fort Randall. You will be prisoners there for punishment."

There was wailing among the women. A roar of surly protest went up among the helpless men. Sitting Bull quieted them all with a wave of his arm.

And about 150 of the Hunkpapas, 30 lodges, were taken more than 200 miles downriver on a fireboat to live under the eyes of the blue-coat soldiers at Fort Randall.

Sitting Bull still had two wives—sisters—Seen By Her Nation and Four Times. His little girl, Standing Holy, who was ten years old, became a pet of the officers at Fort Randall. His oldest surviving son, Crowfoot, was a strange, quiet boy.

The chiefs of the soldiers were stern but decent. In that place there, they said, you can pitch your lodges. There are the trees for wood; there is the water.

The women stared around, satisfied, even pleased. Making camp was their business. They pitched their lodges with a will, helping one another, cutting new lodgepoles in the woods, patching the tattered covers with heavy cloth the officers issued for that purpose. The lodges were in a circle as they always had been since the beginning of time, all with the entrances facing east.

The soldiers issued rations for the Lakota men to claim, each for his own lodge family. The women cooked. Men and boys hunted and snared small game, but never far from camp, because every morning an officer came to count the captive people—154 of them, sometimes less one for a death or plus one for a new baby. This counting was the big event of their day, and they all dressed up for it. There was always a sentry on guard, but otherwise they were free in their camp, on the prairie in warm weather and in the nearby timber during winter.

"We live in a nowhere world," one woman said to another. "We have nothing to do. There is no future." But they did not say this to their men, for whom life was harder, with their occupations gone. The women had their homes and children to look after, and they felt the obligation not to complain. By pretending to be cheerful, they could sometimes make their men feel less like failures.

The children ran and played, no longer afraid of the soldiers, who were sometimes very kind to them. The children learned a few words of English, and the soldiers learned a little Lakota.

Sitting Bull did not change. He was a conquered chief, but still Old Man Chief of the Lakotas. He carried himself proudly. He had never been a jovial man except with his family and close friends; he smiled now no less and no more than before. In Canada he had become a friend of Major Walsh; now he won the grudging respect of the American officers at Fort Randall.

He settled disputes among his people and encouraged

them to be patient in captivity; he himself was a model of patience, and he made a very favorable impression on a young officer, Lieutenant George Ahern, who was assigned to help him with his mail. The chief received mail from all over the world because he was famous. People wrote to ask for his picture or his signature or something he had touched. He had learned to write his name in English, but he could not write anything else and he could not read.

Some of the letters that came to him were in French and German; Lieutenant Ahern could read and write these languages as well as English. The chief had learned the value of money. If someone who wanted his signature sent a dollar, Sitting Bull obliged, so that he could buy tobacco and candy at the little trader's store.

He even developed a little friendly joke with Lieutenant Ahern. The officer gave the chief one of his printed calling cards. Sitting Bull wrote his own name on the back, and whenever he went to see Lieutenant Ahern he took the card along and put it on the officer's table, with a twinkle in his eye.

When Sitting Bull had important visitors, he invited Lieutenant Ahern to be present. There were many visitors, mostly grave chiefs from various parts of the Great Sioux Reservation who had ridden far to bring news, to sit in council, to strengthen their hearts in adversity.

Missionaries from various churches came to see him, too, to try to convert him from his own religion to theirs. He listened carefully when they read from the Bible and translated into the Lakota language, telling him how men must love their neighbors, give all they had to the poor, and sacrifice themselves for others.

Remembering how his own people had always shared both food and famine, how men had gained honor by giving meat or horses to the needy, how every year men had suffered in the Sun-gazing Dance for the good of the whole tribe, Sitting Bull remarked quietly, "The Lakotas were better Christians before they ever heard of Christ than the white men are now."

The missionaries, not understanding anything except that the Lakotas' religion was different from their own, were utterly shocked.

Sitting Bull had some unusual callers one summer day —three Indian children wearing Wasichu clothes, with an old Wasichu woman who tried to boss them around. The chief heard they were coming; his faithful young friend, Standing Tree, brought the news. Standing Tree kept him well informed of what was going on at the fort, as well as he could understand it. The soldiers never paid much attention to him. He just hung around.

Standing Tree reported: "Three children are here from the Indian school way back east somewhere. An old woman is with them, a white woman, very bossy. Their teacher, maybe. They are coming to see you. From the Carlisle school."

"I have heard about that school," the chief replied. "The Wasichu subchief who runs it came out here and persuaded some of the Lakotas to let their children go with him. Chief Spotted Tail, of the Brulés, sent some of his children. But when he visited the school and saw how his children were badly treated, he was very angry and brought them home again."

The two men were silent for a moment, thinking of Spotted Tail—dead now, shot and killed by a long-time enemy, Crow Dog, but that had no connection with the school.

Sitting Bull said, "Maybe I will talk to these people. What do they want?"

"To get more Indian children for the school, but it is not easy, because many died there, and the agents did not even bother to tell the parents."

"Why do they want to see me?"

Standing Tree answered honestly, "Because you are a great chief. The old woman does not know our language. The children are her interpreters, but they don't know enough English. Three years in that school, and they have not learned English! But they are punished every time they speak their own language. There are children of many tribes there. Some do not know the hand sign so they can't even talk to other children."

"I think that is a hard way for children to live," Sitting Bull said. "They have to speak a language that nobody teaches them! Who are these children who are coming to see me?"

"Two boys and a girl. One is an Oglala, the first son of Standing Bear. His name is Plenty Kill. The other boy is a son of Chief American Horse, of the Oglalas. The girl is a daughter of Stands Looking. I don't know anything about her."

Sitting Bull made a motion of dismissal. "I don't care, either. And I do not care to talk to the old woman. But I will talk to one of the boys. Either one."

Standing Tree was embarrassed. "The old woman is very bossy and pompous. She is talking to some officers now. I think they will want you to be polite to her—or else they may punish our people somehow."

Sitting Bull had learned to bend like a young poplar tree in the wind; the wind would pass without harm. The victorious Wasichus called him "wily," with good reason. He smiled now, as he did rarely, and called to his wives:

"An old woman is coming, and some children. I will talk to her a little when I get ready. I want you to make a fuss over her, be very polite, feed her something, act glad to see her. Keep her so busy that she will not bother me. Keep talking. Keep her confused. She does not understand Lakota. Agree with everything she says—but don't let her in until Standing Tree beckons."

Both his wives were amused. They cackled with laughter and began to pull out small things to show the unwelcome white woman.

Sitting Bull added, "Don't forget: the children are *our* people. *They* speak Lakota."

They could hear chatter approaching, with the old woman talking in a shrill voice to one of the officers. Sitting Bull stood in the doorway and shook hands politely with the officer and with the old woman, who squealed and seemed horrified to be touched. They had with them a young half blood to interpret, but the woman talked so much that he did not even try. The officer bowed and departed, looking relieved.

The chief told the interpreter, "Say to the woman that my wives will make her comfortable. I want to talk first to one of the boys." The interpreter made a sign that would have insulted the old woman if she had understood it and pushed a boy forward, saying in Lakota, "The chief will talk to you first. Go inside."

Sitting Bull limped to his bed place and backrest at the back of the lodge and composed himself. The boy remained standing, because he had not been invited to sit down. The chief was favorably impressed.

"What is your real name?" he asked.

"Plenty Kill. At school they call me Luther Standing Bear."

"How many winters have you, boy?"

"Thirteen. For two I have been at the school."

"Why are you here now?"

"Because Captain Pratt thought we could get more children to come. Nobody on the reservation is afraid of us."

"So some people are afraid of *him*. It is said that some children died at the school."

"That is true. They did not say they were sick. They just died. Now those who want to go will have to be looked over first to see if they are well."

"Are the children happy there?" Seeing the boy squirm, the chief glared and reminded him, "A Lakota speaks with a straight tongue."

"They are not all happy. There is a loneliness, a sickness—of the heart. They go there to stay three years, maybe longer."

"Do they learn to speak English and to read and write? Do you speak English well?"

Again the boy squirmed. "No, only a little. The teachers do not know our language, and they punish us if we use it. But we do not speak English well. Not yet."

"Are they training you to be helpful to your people when you come back?"

The boy admitted, "They do not want us to come back. They want us to be like them, to live like them and be farmers. They try to make us civilized."

"Are you going to stay there and be civilized?"

The boy looked startled. "All my life? Oh, no. For a while, maybe. But I don't want to leave my people forever!"

"Do you go to school all the time?"

"Half a day school, half a day we learn a trade. I learn to be a tinsmith. I wanted to learn carpenter work, but they said no. In the summer we work on farms." The boy smiled. "We learn more English there than we do at school."

By the growing racket outside, the chief could tell that his wives were having trouble keeping the old woman occupied. She was very noisy. He told Standing Bear, "You can let the woman come in now."

There was more shrill jabbering from outside after Standing Tree motioned to her. The half-blood interpreter came into the lodge and said in Lakota, "Perhaps the chief will come outside? The woman is afraid of him." He added, grinning, "Maybe she is afraid of rape."

Sitting Bull barely succeeded in keeping from laughing out loud. He looked as friendly as he could when he stepped outside and said, "How."

He even managed to bow.

The woman, suddenly brave, seized his hand and shook it and began to chatter. Once in a while, when she stopped for breath, the interpreter gave a laconic translation of what she had said. It was not worth listening to. When she ran down, Sitting Bull exchanged a few words with the big-eyed children and returned to his lodge.

The woman told about this meeting for the rest of her life when she returned to the East. She described the fearsome, bloody-handed savage as the very soul of gra-

69

ciousness. The children did some private giggling.

What happened during the rest of their visit came to Sitting Bull's camp by moccasin telegraph—messengers, gossip, and some mysterious means of communication that the Wasichus never quite understood. The boy Luther Standing Bear, Plenty Kill, convinced several families that their children should attend Carlisle Indian School. He enlisted his own two brothers and a sister. Robert, son of American Horse, and Maggie, daughter of Stands Looking, went to visit their Oglala families at Pine Ridge Agency, but so many parents there were still in angry mourning for their children who had gone to Carlisle and had died there that the people refused to sacrifice more.

Sitting Bull thought often about the children who had visited him. "I wonder," he said as if to himself, "about their religion. And if they learn enough to fit into the way Wasichus live, if that is what they want. Is it worth the misery, the sickness of the heart? Maybe I could find out something from the children of Spotted Tail of the Brulés. Their agency is at Rosebud."

His faithful follower, Standing Tree, understood what he was being asked to do and answered, "I think you are going to find out."

Standing Tree dropped hints to Indians who came visiting, and the news spread. After a while a young man rode in on a tired horse. He did not have much trouble with the guards, because he was a white man. He ran a store at Rosebud. He would like to see that old rascal Sitting Bull, just for curiosity, he said. The guards could see nothing wrong with that request.

He talked to Standing Tree first. "My name is Charlie

Tackett," he said in English. Then in Lakota, smiling, "I do not need an interpreter. I *am* an interpreter. My wife is Red Road. She is the daughter of Spotted Tail. Both of us were at the Carlisle School. Does Sitting Bull want to talk to me?"

"He wants to talk to you," Standing Tree replied fervently.

That was how Sitting Bull found out what he wanted to know. The two talked for the rest of the day, and the young man spent the night in the lodge. Sitting Bull's wives served the best food they could from the rations that their jailers issued.

This is the story Charles Tackett told the imprisoned Chief Sitting Bull:

"The soldier who runs the school is named Captain Pratt. He came out here to get Lakota boys and girls for his school, but the parents would not let them go. It is far away, and they love their children. The children did not want to go, either. They were afraid.

"Chief Spotted Tail refused, with the other fathers, but then he thought it would be good if Lakotas could speak English and read it, not depending on men with forked tongues to tell them what is said on the paper-that-talks.

"Spotted Tail decided to send four of his own sons, the oldest eighteen years old, the youngest nine, and a grandson and a granddaughter. He sent also my wife, his daughter Red Road—she was eighteen then —to look after them, and he made Captain Pratt hire me to be interpreter at the school. I was paid and so was my wife. She did not want to go at all. When she was younger, he wanted to make her go to a school

71

far away, run by Catholic nuns, but she ran away from home that time.

"When the Carlisle school had been running for a while, several Lakota chiefs were sent to Washington to talk to the President, the Grandfather. Spotted Tail was one of them. They stopped at the school to see how their children were getting along, and they were very angry. None of the children had learned English, but Pratt had a man to punish them if they spoke their own language. They could not read or write. They were not proud any more—they were afraid all the time. Pratt did not like me or my wife Red Road because sometimes the children came to us when they felt very bad. They were miserable and sick at heart for home.

"Spotted Tail and Captain Pratt had a very big argument. The Lakota boys were not learning anything that would help them when they came back here—Pratt does not want any of the children to come back and be Indians. He wants them to turn into white people and live that way."

Sitting Bull asked, "Do the children want to do that?"

"Very few, I think. Luther Standing Bear may try it, out of curiosity, and some others, but they will come home."

"Spotted Tail brought his children home, didn't he?"

"Of course. He was very angry. Pratt fired me from my job as interpreter, so of course my wife came back with me. Pratt said the children would learn English faster if they had to learn it, without me to talk for them."

"It is a good thing to know English, but that school does not seem good. Pratt seems like a cruel man."

"He is," Charlie Tackett agreed. "He is an army captain, not a teacher. I taught the boys some English when he wasn't listening. But I know Lakota. Their teachers don't. The boys and girls learn more in the summer, when they work on farms and live with farmers' families."

"We need schools for our children," the chief said thoughtfully, "but with better teachers."

"There are some schools on the reservation now," Tackett told him, "with bad teachers. They are relatives of the agents, who give them jobs."

When Charlie Tackett was ready to leave, the chief said, "I thank you for telling me these things. You speak with a straight tongue. I do not like to shake hands with white men, but you are a Lakota."

Tackett knew that the Old Man Chief of the Lakotas could not have paid him a greater compliment.

As time passed, it seemed to Sitting Bull's people that they were going to live in this nowhere world of captivity until they died. They endured from one day to the next. Older people grieved, remembering how life used to be and ought to be, but small children were satisfied enough, not knowing any better. They had enough to eat; their parents loved them. But they had no ambition —why aim the arrow when there is no target?

One day Brings Horses talked about these things to her man, saying, "In the old days, when our camps moved often, my mother could visit the platforms where the loved dead ones rested. She used to tell their spirits in the Land of Many Lodges what was happening in this world. Then she cried a little, and it comforted her. But we can never go back to the tree where we put her body, and our baby boy's body, when we were trying to find the Medicine Line."

"That is true," Elk Rising agreed. "We can't go there or anywhere."

"But I could talk to my mother anyway," Brings Horses said thoughtfully. "I could go up in the woods tomorrow and tell her about everything, and maybe she will hear me. I could go right after the soldier counts all our people. If someone could keep Wakan Woman busy so she does not follow me, and tell other people to stay away from me."

"I think you should do that. The children and the rest of us will watch the *wakan* Nez Percé woman and keep her busy somehow."

So the next morning, after the counting, Brings Horses Woman went quietly into the woods, with nobody watching, and sat under a big tree, pretending its branches held the death platform of her mother, Whirlwind. She cried a little, not howling or making any other noise of grief, and made one cut on her left arm, just above the scar from the bullet wound, as a special token of mourning—but where her sleeve would cover it. Then she talked to the spirit of her mother.

"You are happy there, I know, and honored among your people, as you always were. I don't do great things, but taking pride in your example, I do little things. I won't bother you with any of that now.

"Maybe I should not bother you at all, but tell my baby I love him and we will meet sometime."

She thought for a little while. "We are living a nothing life, not bad, not good. The spirit of the people is not broken. It is feeble, like a fire almost

74

burned out. The grandmothers still tell the children the stories they must know, about religion and the brave deeds of warriors—and how you were brave, rescuing a baby from a grizzly bear. Girls must know that they can be brave. Boys still play games to test their fortitude and courage—but what use is it? They can't earn honor as in the old days.

"When the soldiers ration out beef, the boys and the men hunt down the animals—nothing like buffalo. These are thin, slow, stumbling cattle of the white men. Young girls help us butcher, so they learn a little, but we can't teach them our important skills of tanning and quilling, because there are so few hides, and porcupines are hard to find.

"There is not much joy in living any more, with nothing to give away. We do not dare carry out the sacred Gazing-at-the-Sun Dance. The white people would watch and not understand. On the reservation they can do it, far from the agencies, but we are at a fort, a soldier town.

"Morals are not as strict as they should be. Our young women do not wear chastity ropes until they marry, as I did, as you did, and all our grandmothers. We are not bad people yet, but we are becoming weak. The evil spirits are winning."

She broke down then and wept for her people, their glorious past and their cloudy future. Then she walked slowly back, with her thin shoulders bowed, to the prison camp. She did not feel better for having talked to the gallant spirit of Whirlwind. She only felt ashamed.

She might have felt better if she had known of a conversation that was going on in the commanding officer's quarters at Fort Randall at that moment. A white man, no longer young, faced the commanding officer and spoke with determination.

"You know me, sir?"

"Of course, Andy. You fought in the Civil War, then you came west and you've lived among the Sioux for years. Your wife is a Sioux."

"And I speak the language. These people trust me, because I never lie to them. If I ask the old warriors questions, they generally answer—and they answer straight."

"I believe you," the officer assured him. "What's your problem, Andy? Or did you come to solve mine?"

"I've worked up a mad ever since this bunch of Hunkpapas were moved in here as prisoners. They don't deserve the treatment they're getting. Don't get huffy—you can't help it. But there's no reason for them to be prisoners."

The officer frowned. "Orders from the War Department."

"Because some damn fool back East thinks Sitting Bull himself killed General Custer at the Little Big Horn. Thousands of damn fools think so. So he's being punished, with his people." Old Andy was working up to real anger; it had taken him a long time to decide to face the officer on this matter.

"I don't care if everybody in Washington from President Arthur on down thinks Sitting Bull personally killed General Custer at the Little Big Horn. He did not! He didn't even cross the river. Every warrior I've talked to says he did not! He wasn't supposed to fight in that battle —he had a grown son who did, and the young men

76

resented it if the older braves with lots of war honors got in and took some glory *they* could get.

"Anyhow, Sitting Bull urged them on with brave-up shouts, made their hearts big, while he helped the women get ready to escape—his mother was one of them. He knew what was going on, all right, but he didn't kill Custer. Remember, he was all used up from that Sun Dance he'd been in not long before. Why, most of them didn't even know which white soldier *was* General Custer until they heard about it later. They called him Long Hair, but before that campaign he'd had his hair cut short.

"So if killing Custer is what the chief is being kept prisoner for, it's a damn injustice and you ought to let him go."

The officer replied, "I believe you. Now excuse me. I want to send some telegrams and write some letters to my superiors."

*   *   *

And so, by order of the War Department, Sitting Bull and his camp of Hunkpapa Lakotas were loaded onto a fireboat early in May of 1883 and moved upriver to be with their relatives and friends at Standing Rock, on the west bank of the Missouri River.

On the way, Wakan Woman, the mad Nez Percé, jumped off the steamboat and was drowned. Brings Horses screamed and wanted to jump and try to save her, but Elk Rising held his wife's arms firmly and reminded her, "She has not really been in this world for a long time. Let her leave it."

Two young men, good swimmers, did go over the side but could not find the body. The steamboat men, cursing, slowed and threw ropes so the young men could save themselves.

Brings Horses stood looking down at the muddy river. Her husband was puzzled; he said, "There are tears on your cheeks. Do you really mourn that her troubles are ended?"

"Nobody will mourn for her or miss her," Brings Horses answered. "That is why there are tears on my cheeks."

PART III

HELP THE PEOPLE!

1883

7

The Snake Vision

The fireboat carrying Sitting Bull and his followers up
the Missouri from their imprisonment at Fort Randall let
them off at the soldier town of Fort Yates, and soldiers
marched beside them as they walked (or rode, for a few
had horses) to Standing Rock Agency.

Their agent, a sour man, young but with white hair,
lectured them there. His name was McLaughlin.

Stormy whispered to his father, "Why does he hate us?
The soldiers where we used to live did not."

Elk Rising did not answer while White Hair was talking
but watched him carefully. Later he explained quietly, "I
think it is Sitting Bull he hates. He scowled more when
he looked at the chief. He did not speak to Sitting Bull
like one chief to another. He pretended that Sitting Bull
is nobody."

White Hair was married to a half-Santee woman and
knew some of the Lakota language, but he spoke through
an interpreter in a very bossy way:

"You can live in a place by the Grand River. It is about
forty miles from here. Every two weeks, on Saturday, the

81

head man of each family must come here to Standing Rock to pick up rations. You will learn to be farmers, like civilized people. I will send men to help you get started, and your Grandfather in Washington will give you some horses and other livestock to help you. You will have to hurry about hoeing and planting crops, because it is already late in the season."

So they settled along the Grand River. Sitting Bull had two cabins and a corral for stock; a few other men had cabins that carpenters built or let them help build, but most of the people lived in conical lodges of coarse, heavy cloth because they could not get buffalo hides any more. The last great buffalo hunt had taken place the year before.

The old men sang sadly to their drums, because so much of this was wrong. A camp circle should be round, not strung out far apart; a lodge should be round, because round was good. The Lakota nation was seen as a round shape, a hoop without end or beginning. But a cabin with square corners broke the sacred pattern. Besides, it could not be moved, like a lodge, when the place around it became dirty with trash. Ah, so many bad changes, breaking ancient custom! And it was wrong to tear up the skin of their mother, the earth, with their hoes, so as to plant grain. But they gashed her skin and prayed to her to forgive them.

Even Sitting Bull learned to use a hoe and worked along with his wives and was patient in adversity. His people were ashamed to see him do work that their fathers would not have let even women do. But the chief did not act ashamed. He said, "We will do what we must do."

All during their imprisonment at Fort Randall, Sitting Bull's people had kept the past alive for themselves and their children by telling the old stories about religion and their brave ancestors. They kept hope alive that way, too, not knowing whether it was really any use, because they had no promise that their imprisonment would ever end. The grandmothers told the little ones, and the men who had been warriors still recounted their own brave deeds for everyone to remember.

In the lodge of Elk Rising, where there was no grand-mother, his wife Brings Horses Woman told the stories to the three children; her son Stormy, her adopted son Saved Her Cub, and her daughter Red Pipe Girl. Brings Horses told often of the splendid courage of her mother, Whirlwind, and set her up as an example of a great, good woman.

Elk Rising had said once to the children, "Whirlwind was brave indeed, but do not forget your own mother. Pull up your sleeve, my woman, and show them the scar." Brings Horses did so but bowed her head, embarrassed at the attention.

"My mother did great things. I only do small things," she said.

"Children, see the bullet scar on her arm? She was wounded by blue-coat soldiers when she helped make meat when we went south into this country for buffalo while we lived in Grandmother England's Land. But she did not even fall from her horse, and when the bullet was dug from the wound she did not cry out. That is the kind of mother you have. Never forget!"

Brings Horses told them, "See the scars on your father's chest and back? Those are from times he suffered in the Sun-gazing Dance, thanking Wakan Tanka and praying for the good of all our people."

"Will we dance before Wakan Tanka when we are older?" asked Saved Her Cub, who was ten.

Elk Rising looked very grim as he replied, "How can I know that? It has always been so, but the Wasichus are changing so many things. There is no guessing what they will do to us."

Stormy, fourteen, was able to hang around conversations unnoticed where a man could not go without invitation. He never seemed to be listening, but he always was, and he picked up considerable information.

"In some places the dance is still held," he said briefly but would not tell how he knew. He had heard messengers report to Sitting Bull—who was well aware that he had heard and wanted the news to be known without official announcement. The chief knew it would be a comfort to his fellow prisoners to realize that this most important of the Lakotas' religious ceremonies was still going on once a year.

For the prisoners, many customs could not be carried out because they were so closely watched. In all the two years they were at Fort Randall, no youth went out to lament on a hill, to starve and thirst and pray to the spirits for medicine power. This took from two to four days, depending on how long the suppliant vowed to suffer, and nobody could be gone from camp that long because of the daily roll call.

One of the first things the older people thought of when they learned that they were going to Standing Rock Agency, to have a place of their own like other Lakotas, was that they would be able to worship properly again.

But many of the younger ones really did not care. Even after they settled down on Grand River, and Sitting Bull sent messages to other chiefs among the Hunkpapas to settle on a time and place for the sacred Sun-gazing Dance, the boys were not excited.

Stormy asked a young man five years older than himself, "Is anyone in your family going to vow and dance?"

"What's the use?" the young man said. "There is nothing to look forward to."

Stormy boasted, "My father's brother, White Mountain, has vowed, even though it will be very hard on him because he was crippled with a shot in the hip when we were fighting to reach Canada. He will have buffalo skulls hanging from the skin of his back. He is a brave man. . . . Are you going out to lament for medicine power soon?"

The young man sneered. "That was good for men who would be hunters and warriors. What use is medicine power to me? There are no buffalo to hunt, and we are puny before our enemies, so we cannot fight. The Wasichus have all the power. Except what is in guns—but we have no guns any more."

Stormy did not feel that he could talk to anyone about this great problem, but his heart believed that there *was* some value in the old ways.

The Sun-gazing Dance of 1883 was never held at Standing Rock after all, nor at any other agency except Pine Ridge, where Brings Horses' brother and his family were. It was not held there after that.

Every two weeks the heads of families had to go to Standing Rock Agency for rations from the government —for each person so much beef, bacon, flour, and coffee, sometimes some clothing. Earlier, the chiefs had received the rations and handed them out to the people, but White Hair, the agent at Standing Rock, did not let the chiefs have any honor unless they were yes-yes chiefs who agreed with everything he said. Even these he did not permit to give out rations to their people. So every man from Grand River had to travel the forty miles by wagon to claim food for his own lodge.

On one of these trips soon after Sitting Bull's people arrived, White Hair made known the terrible new rules from the government in Washington, listing what he called "Indian offenses." All these were now offenses:

A man having two or more wives. He could have only one and must throw away any others.

All feasts and dances were forbidden—those traditional ways of getting together with friends.

Medicine priests could no longer give help to the sick or the heartsick or aid them when they wanted to come closer to the Great Mystery in worship.

A man could no longer ask for a girl he wanted to marry by leaving gifts at the door of her father. The Wasichus thought this was the same as buying the girl, not understanding that the gift brought her honor.

Nobody could mourn by destroying his own property.

There could be no Sun-gazing Dance. The Wasichus saw only the bloody self-torture in the dance, not the courage, not the great love that renewed the spiritual life of the people and made them strong. The Wasichus did not understand that if one sacrifices material things to the Great Mystery, Wakan Tanka, one only gives them back to their original source, but a man's body is his own, and his pain is the only thing that is really his to give Wakan Tanka.

These new rules indeed crushed the spirit of the people. Not worship the Great Holy? Not give thanks or plead for help? No. Forbidden. Men who had the scars of honor on their chests or backs—some had both—took to going naked from the waist up so the grieving people could see the scars and remember and hope again. The people took heart from seeing the great scars on the body of Sitting Bull, who had danced many times while praying for his nation; their hearts lifted at the sight of the hundred small scars on his arms, fifty on each arm. Those scars reminded them of the time he had vowed and given one hundred pieces of his own flesh and had had his great vision of enemy soldiers falling dead into their camp, just before the Battle of the Little Bighorn.

All their old customs were wrong now, the government said. Whatever they did that was different from the way the white men did was wrong. The women could not gash their arms and legs in proper mourning, and everyone was too poor to show the old respect to the dead by giving away goods.

But how could men throw away their extra wives? Who would take care of them? There was no place for them to go, and they had done no wrong. So some men lied and claimed that one wife was a widowed sister or a cousin.

Sitting Bull himself made a joke of the order: "Get me a white woman for a wife and I will throw away the two I have," he said. This shocked the white men, and Sitting Bull still had his two wives when he was killed.

There was helpless rage among the conquered Lakotas at these changes, but all they could do was submit. If a few met and drummed and prayed sorrowfully to the Great Mystery, how was White Hair the agent going to know it? Of course he had his Lakota policemen, men who had turned their backs on their own people. But they were not likely to tell about someone just praying, because they did not quite dare turn their backs on the Great Mystery.

Stormy spent much of his time on the edges of groups of men who talked about the old days, about buffalo hunts and battles and stealing horses from their ancient enemies, the Crow tribe, about good times and bad times, and about brave men who were dead. They talked of long-ago camps in a vast country that had been theirs, and of fording rivers that Stormy would never see. When they talked about their vision quests and terrifying experiences in receiving power from the spirits, he listened even harder.

Almost always his adopted brother was near him, silent as a shadow. Saved Her Cub *was* his shadow, uninvited, even when Stormy, four years older, wanted to be alone to think very hard about a matter he could not get out of his mind.

When they had lived on Grand River for a year and Stormy had counted fifteen winters in his life, he spoke very firmly one day to Saved Her Cub: "Go somewhere for a little while. I want to talk to my father."

He and Elk Rising sauntered to the river's edge and sat down.

"Father," he said abruptly, "I want to go on a hill and lament for a medicine dream."

Elk Rising put his arm around the boy's shoulders and thought for a long time, looking at the water. Finally he said, "It is good. I will do everything I can to help you. But it will be harder for you than it was for me, long ago when we were free to worship and pray to the spirits. Because now it is an offense, and the ritual must be carried out in secret. The Metal Breasts are the eyes and ears of White Hair the agent."

He thought some more. "I will go now and talk to old Heavy Eagle, the holy man. You can tell your mother. She will be proud."

They walked back to the village together.

When Elk Rising went to the ragged lodge of the old holy man he carried a sacred pipe, because he was going to beg for help, but it was hidden under his blanket, not held before him in both hands as was proper. He spoke quietly to Heavy Eagle, whose eyes widened as he agreed, "I will smoke with you," thus promising to do whatever thing was asked. "Few people ask me any more."

They sat down in the lodge, with the old man's wife on guard outside, and offered the pipe to the Powers of the six directions, sky, earth, west, north, east, and south.

"Yes, I will go with you and your son," the holy man promised. "The sweat bath beforehand should be no problem. Sweat baths are not forbidden. Bring two or three men you can trust, and we will not sing the special prayers loudly. Your other boy can stay outside to warn us if anyone comes who should not know.

"We will ride far to a hill where nobody goes, and leave the boy on it for—how many days did he choose?"

"Three days."

"I will teach him the ritual and then we will go away, returning after three days. During that time I will sing prayers for him in the special language of holy priests. Metal Breasts do not understand it. Neither do you, or anyone but a man trained as a priest.

"Day after tomorrow we will begin with the purification, the sweat bath."

Elk Rising bowed his head. "When I went out to seek my dream, my father gave the priest a good horse. I have no horse to give you, only a kettle of stew from my lodge."

Heavy Eagle replied with dignity, "I accept the fine gift."

Both men wondered why the boy wanted to do this thing, but they did not ask him. It was enough that he wished to follow the old way, although no power from spirits would help him as a hunter when there were no buffalo to hunt, and no power would strengthen his courage in battle when there could be no battles for a defeated people. But Stormy himself knew why he needed spiritual help. His knowledge was all that mattered.

He was very much afraid, as thousands and thousands of boys had been afraid before him. He went ahead anyway, as they had done. He remembered hearing stories about the terrible experience of his Grandmother Whirlwind's uncle, Grey Bull, who, after he was a successful warrior, had dreamed of Thunder Beings and had to become a holy clown, a *heyoka,* forever poor, with great spiritual gifts but meeker than the smallest ant. Stormy hoped he would not have to be a Thunder Dreamer, but it was a dangerous chance that he had to take.

When the chosen day came, Stormy and his father, with the holy man and three or four other older men who could be trusted, entered a sweat lodge and purified their bodies and souls, praying constantly. The boy Saved Her Cub kept watch outside. The sweat lodge was not forbidden, but the holy songs were. One man sang a song about his own vision of a spotted eagle. After the long, solemn ceremony of prayer, Stormy was given a drink of water—all he wanted. This was the last water he would drink until the vision quest was finished three days later.

Wearing moccasins, a breechclout, and a blanket, and carrying a sacred pipe before him, he rode a horse; his father and the priest led horses loaded with sacred sage and offering sticks. At the foot of the high hill chosen by the priest, Stormy waited, praying pitifully, loudly, to all the spirits, especially to Wakan Tanka, who *is* all the spirits.

His father and the priest continued up the hill and did the necessary things: they made him a bed of sage, and set up a center post and four other posts. They returned to Stormy, and he climbed the hill alone, stark naked, without moccasins or breechclout but carrying the blanket, which he could use at night.

Before the spirits, a man was nothing. All the way up the hill, he cried, "Wakan Tanka, be merciful to me that my people may live!"

He prayed at the center pole, then at the pole at the west, and back at the center again, constantly moving from one to another, but always returning to the center. He prayed to the sky and all the spirits, sometimes aloud, sometimes in silence, always with his whole heart, but trying also to be alert for messengers that might come from the Great Holy in any guise. An insect, a bird, an animal large or small—anything might be a messenger, and it might speak or simply pass by.

When he was tired out, he sat down on the bed of sage, leaning against the center pole, crying, "Wakan Tanka, be merciful to me that I may help the people to live!" When he was exhausted, he slept fitfully.

He heard the small night sounds of unseen wings and tiny, scurrying feet, but no messenger spoke. On the third night of hunger, thirst, and constant fear the vision came.

He had been sleeping a little, lying on the bed of sage. He awoke and cried, "Be merciful that I may help the people to live!" His voice was hardly more than a whisper, but it grew to many voices, howling and wailing around him in the night, echoing his cry, *Help the people to live! Help the people to live! Help the people . . . help the people. . . .*"

It was an endless, sickening repetition of his own frantic prayer, dwindling as his mind whirled and his body shook from cold and exhaustion.

The last echo was an anguished whisper: *Help the people!*

This was not what he had prayed for, a promise of power. It was a command. And he was helpless, as man should admit he is helpless before the Great Mystery.

He lay there bewildered with the world whirling but becoming visible in the dawnlight. He was motionless, belly down on the blanket-covered sage, with his head turned to one side. As close as the length of his arm, a snake was looking at him, flicking its long tongue. He stared back, moving only his eyelids, looking into the face of death.

The snake did not coil to strike or make any rattling sound with its tail. It only looked at him, sticking out its tongue. Then it turned and undulated away, and he dared to breathe again.

Stormy pulled himself to a sitting position and called after the rattlesnake, "But you did not tell me how to help the people!" His mouth was so dry that he could not form the words properly.

No voice came to explain. He heard no sacred song to learn. He lay down again, weeping.

Pretty soon his father came, and the old holy man with him. The vow of lamenting for three days was finished. Elk Rising wrapped his son tenderly in the blanket, and the holy man held a can of water for him to drink. Stormy drank, then pushed the can away, dismayed.

"But this is not right!" he objected. "No water until I tell my experiences to the wise old men. That is how it was when you went out to dream for a protector."

The priest explained sadly, "Everything is different now. Drink more. You cannot ride into camp without water—you are too used up. Someone might notice. One of the Metal Breasts might see you and tell White Hair that you were following the old religion. Here, drink more. When we ride in, you must sit your horse strongly, and we will be only three men not worth noticing."

The wise men who would judge Stormy's dream and, he hoped, explain it were waiting. Chief Sitting Bull was among them, not only to do him honor (it was long since a youth had gone out to lament to the Great Mystery!) but also because he himself had had visions of great import.

The men in council were impressed by Stormy's story

but very much puzzled. Some of them put their right hands over their mouths and said, *"Wakan! Wakan!"*

While they considered, Stormy felt his stomach sink. He said, "Grandfathers, I have just remembered something. It was pale in my memory, and only now it came back. After the snake turned and left without harming me, I knew someone else was near, a friend to me. The snake struck him, and I wanted to mourn."

The old men murmured. All of them had lamented for a vision. They knew how a memory could be pale and then return vividly.

One asked, "The snake had a forked tongue that darted at you?"

"Yes, it was forked."

There was a murmur of understanding. One of the hand-sign names for "white man" was the same as "forked tongue, liar."

Someone said, "Maybe the snake was not your protector but a warning spirit."

The old priest suggested, "A white man who lies but does not hurt him because it is not yet his time? The person it strikes is someone he cannot see because he does not know him yet?"

"How can I help the people?" Stormy pleaded. "That was the command of the voice and the echoes in the sky."

Sitting Bull spoke quietly: "Every brave man who endures helps the people by his example. This is how it is now, as the white man tries to make us walk his road."

There was a deep growl of agreement. The old men considered Stormy's problem further. Spirit messages were often not clear, so on the chance that the snake might be a protector they advised the vision-seeker to consider it his helper and to think often about the command, trying to understand how he could carry it out: *Help the people!*

So he killed a rattlesnake one day, apologizing and explaining to its spirit, as was proper, and kept with him always its rattle with seven buttons. He had honor among those of his people who knew what had happened, those who could be trusted not to inform the Metal Breasts.

Members of his family were very proud of him.

Saved Her Cub was still his shadow, but walked a little behind him now, doing him honor. Stormy told him of the vision of Death that looked him in the face, although it had not seemed like a vision; it seemed real. He told him, too, of the terrible echo: *Help the people! Help the people!*

"But nobody understands what it means that I should do," he said sorrowfully. "How can I obey the command when I do not understand it?"

Sometimes he sat by himself, away from the camp, and made music with a small drum while he sang to the spirits:

> "A voice in the sky commands me,
> A great voice speaking commands me.
> All you above and below and around, help me,
> Help me to understand the meaning.
> Death looked at me but did not speak."

8

Home Without Love

Elk Rising, that once-proud warrior, tried hard to be a farmer. Stormy worked beside him; so did Saved Her Cub when they could catch him. The family had a pig to raise; they had never learned to like the taste of pork, but it was meat. Looking after the pig was the job of Saved Her Cub. Brings Horses Woman had a few chickens that she kept tame by feeding them in front of the lodge and by talking to them softly. Her daughter, Red Pipe Girl, helped by finding where they laid their eggs. But she was a willful child, and Brings Horses sighed about her, not knowing how to bring up a daughter in this dreary new world where the skills she herself had learned when she was young were of no value.

The most exciting times were when the agency issued a beef ration on the hoof. Then everybody made the forty-mile trip to Standing Rock and camped there. The men chased the cattle, yelling, and killed them, pretending these stodgy, scrawny beasts were the quick-moving, dangerous buffalo that were gone now. The women butchered them, the agent's men weighed the meat (not very much for each family), and the people could dream of the old, free days.

They barely lived, because sometimes the government did not send as much food as promised, and the crops were never good—too little rain came.

Whenever they went to the agency, Stormy watched keenly what the men who worked there did. Those white men or half bloods who could speak Lakota as well as English were useful and had jobs that paid money. If they could read and write and work with numbers and money, they had jobs. Education was a good thing, he understood. He picked up a few English words to add to those he had learned at Fort Randall.

One night he awoke from a sound sleep and sat up in his bed place, suddenly understanding the command he had received in his vision: *Help the people! Help the people!* He lay down again and thought about it, not sleeping any more.

Next day he asked Standing Tree, his older adopted brother who was the faithful worshiper of Sitting Bull, "Can you get permission from the chief for me to talk to him?"

Standing Tree stared. "Probably. But why?"

"I want to ask his advice. There is a school far away to the eastward for Indians. I want to go there."

"The chief knows about that school," Standing Tree told him. "You can talk to him now. Don't you want to talk to your father first?"

Stormy shook his head. "Later."

The chief was standing in front of one of his cabins, looking into the distance, looking grim. He wore a blanket wrapped around like a skirt but was naked from the waist up. He glanced at the young man and nodded permission to speak.

Standing Tree said, "My adopted brother Stormy would like to talk to you."

"He is welcome," the chief replied. "Come in, Stormy, son of Elk Rising."

Standing Tree, not invited, did not enter.

Sitting Bull sat down in the lodge master's place and beckoned Stormy to sit beside him but did not offer a pipe. He waited.

"I went out to dream last summer," Stormy began, "and a voice commanded me. But I did not understand it."

"I know," the chief reminded him. "Our young men do not often do that any more. Why did you?"

"Because I believe the old way is right. I wanted help from the Great Mystery."

"I hoped that was the reason. The command you received was *Help the people.* I do not understand it either."

"I think I understand it now. Suddenly understanding came. I think it means I should go to the school for Indians far away to the eastward and be educated. Then I might be able to help the people in dealing with the white man."

Sitting Bull looked at him for a long time. "I cannot read or write. It is as if I were blind sometimes in arguing with the government men. They keep wanting to take away more of our reservation land; they try to divide us, they frighten some of the chiefs into signing papers. Those chiefs are blind, too, because the papers do not always say truly what the government men promise. I wish I could read and write and talk straight to the gov-

ernment men in their own language without an interpreter who may lie or leave out something. Then I could
fight better to save our lands and help the people."

Stormy held his breath. Sitting Bull continued:

"What have you heard about that school far away?"

Stormy shivered in spite of himself. "I heard that some
boys and girls die there."

The chief said, "That is true."

"The people who run the school are cruel. They want
the Indians to stay in the East forever and become just
like themselves. But some come back here. I do not know
whether what they learned helps the people very much.
But if a man wanted to help, he would have a beginning."

"Do you remember," the chief asked, "the children
who visited me at Fort Randall, the two boys and a girl
from that school? Yes, of course you do. The school no
longer wants small children like those. The school wants
big boys and girls, young men and women, for three
years. Are you not afraid?"

Stormy looked at the scarred body of Sitting Bull, at
the lumpy scars on his chest, marks of honor proving he
had undergone the torture of the Sun-gazing Dance, and
the row of small scars on each arm.

Stormy drew in his breath and answered honestly,
"Yes, I am afraid. But I think I should go."

The chief laid his rough hand on Stormy's arm. "It is
all right to be afraid. I have been afraid, but I went ahead
anyway when I knew I was doing the right thing. It is the
same with your father and all warriors, and with many
Lakota women. Your Grandmother Whirlwind, that
great woman whom I never met, it must have been the
same with her."

Stormy whispered, "*You* were afraid?"

"Not of death, not for a long time. A young man in his first battle may fear death but pretends he does not. We all pretend. I am always afraid of the Powers. That is right, and it is proper to let them know it. That is why we lament. You know what fear is. But before everyone except the Powers you can pretend otherwise.

"You cannot suffer in the Sun-gazing Dance, because it is forbidden. But I think you will suffer in another way if you go to school, and you will have no scars to prove your courage. The scars will be in your heart. When that suffering comes to you, remember us and endure, endure."

The chief stood up, dismissing him. "Now you must go and talk to your parents, because they will suffer, too. And let me remind you, the agent at Standing Rock may try to discourage you, because you are of my people. But he has orders to find a certain number of young men and women for the school, so he will take you, I think."

First Stormy told his father. Elk Rising was appalled but did not argue. He laid his hand on Stormy's shoulder and said, "You must tell your mother in some way that will not break her heart. But there is no way! Come."

Brings Horses was spreading ragged clothing she had just washed on some brush to dry in the sun. Elk Rising himself told her, and she wailed as if for someone dead.

"How long will you be gone?" was the first thing she asked.

"Three winters and summers," Stormy told her. "That is how long it takes before I can come home."

She wailed again. Then she became the daughter of Whirlwind, who had been able to remember even when she was suffering that the spirit of the people must not be broken.

"I have two pairs of new moccasins for you," she said. "And a good blanket, a decent shirt, white man's pants from the clothing issue to fit you. I will get you some jerked beef to eat on the way to the agency. It will take you more than one day walking."

He did not have to walk, after all. A man was going with a team and wagon. The last Stormy saw of his family, his parents, his older adopted brother Standing Tree, his younger adopted brother (his shadow, who adored him) Saved Her Cub, and his sister were waving from in front of their lodge. And he saw the chief, Sitting Bull, hold up his arm in a kind of farewell salute.

At the agency, one Lakota policeman told him to go away. Another policeman came and listened to him and made fun of him: "You say you *want* to go away to school! You must be lying."

"I speak with a straight tongue," Stormy replied. "Do you?"

He spent the morning arguing with one haughty man after another until Agent McLaughlin himself came scowling to see what the fuss was about. Now indeed Stormy understood how useful it would be if he could talk English and not have to depend on others to interpret, although McLaughlin could speak some Lakota.

They humiliated him; McLaughlin said he was too old, they wanted younger boys. But the fact was that the agent had not filled his quota of children to go, and secretly he was glad to have a willing volunteer, although he was suspicious, too. This was one of Sitting Bull's hostiles. To get this earnest, determined boy as a volunteer for the school would be a triumph for McLaughlin.

When the day was over, Stormy had been accepted and was bitterly unhappy. His left hand was cramped, because all day he had clutched in it the symbol of his medicine power, the rattles of a snake like the one that had passed him by when he lay on the hill and heard the echoes howl *Help the people!*

Two dozen boys and three girls were herded aboard a fireboat at Fort Yates, wearing the best (or only) clothes they had and carrying their few possessions—a blanket apiece, extra moccasins, a few keepsakes, some jerky or *wasna,* pemmican, to eat. A missionary woman was with them to protect the girls. The boys slept, but not very well, on the hard deck—harder than the ground—with their sleep light because of fear and the noise and shaking of the fireboat. More Lakota children boarded the fireboat on later stops.

Stormy became acquainted with some of the boys. All of them boasted just a little about themselves. Stormy especially liked a boy of his own age, Takes Much, an Oglala from Pine Ridge Agency. His father's name was Scatters Them.

Stormy told him quietly, "I have relatives at Pine Ridge, my mother's brother Morning Rider and his family. My mother was an Oglala. But my father is Hunkpapa, and we live with Sitting Bull's band."

"I know Morning Rider's sons!" Takes Much exclaimed. "Hawk Child and Kills Grizzly and She Throws Him. Maybe we will learn fast to write letters so I can tell my parents that you are here and they can tell your uncle and his family."

"We have not had any word of them for a long time," Stormy told him. "They came back from Canada before we did, and we were prisoners at Fort Randall for two years before we went to Grand River."

Ah, it was good to have a friend among strangers!

They all disembarked at a town, and the missionary woman said good-bye, and a man who could speak a little Lakota took over her duties as chaperon. He assigned the oldest girl to look after the younger ones.

When they got off the fireboat, everybody on the street stared at them, and some people jeered, as they walked along. Their white-man leader took them to a building where long tables were set with plates, knives and forks and spoons, and told them to sit on benches.

The Indian youths did not bother to sit on the benches. There was food in big bowls and platters on the tables, and all of them were half starved. They raced to the tables and scooped food into their blankets (the lumps of sugar in the bowls were a great prize) and ran outside to eat it.

Stormy and Takes Much, taller than most of the others, appointed themselves policemen to make sure the girls and the smaller boys got their share. As the children ate, townspeople gathered around to watch and laugh at their hunger.

From this place they were herded to a row of little houses connected together and standing on long iron strips. Stormy and Takes Much got in front of the procession, just behind the white leader, and made a dance of the journey. Takes Much had little bells on the fringes of his leggings, so he jingled music and the younger children laughed and lost some of their fear.

They all climbed into the long row of houses and found the inside very grand, with rows of soft seats covered with green material. There was an aisle down the middle, with two seats on each side from one end to the other. Everybody had a hilarious time bouncing on the seats and changing places and staring out through the glass windows.

. . . Until the whole thing began, after much noise up front, to move! The Lakotas and the few Cheyennes with them were terrified. Few of them had ever seen a train. None of them had ever ridden on one.

Smaller children began to wail, clutching their seats with both hands. Stormy and Takes Much, remembering the brave-up songs of their fathers, tried to change what they recalled.

The leader, whom they called Mister, became impatient and cross.

They lived through days and uncomfortable nights on the train heading east. They had to sleep sitting up. The name of the school, Carlisle, they had heard, but they had never heard of the State of Pennsylvania, never guessed how far away any place could be.

One of the hardest things for the new pupils to get used to was that at the school there was no family love. This was something that all of them had taken for granted, including those who were orphans and had been adopted into families. Captain Richard Pratt, who ran the school, liked to be told by ladies of visiting church groups that he was like a father to all the children —and indeed when visitors were present, he gave that impression. Furthermore, he really thought he was. But he was not an Indian, he was a white man and an army officer, and he was more stern and fault-finding than any of their Indian fathers had ever been.

Another hard thing for the children was to be hungry

and not be allowed to eat even though they knew there was plenty of food. One of the first things the new pupils learned was that the time, not the appetite, governed eating. They learned very soon to tell time, although most of them had not known what clocks were for.

The sun's position had been all the clock they needed, but here they were punished for going outside to look at it when they were supposed to be doing something else.

Lakota boys near Stormy's age could still remember dimly the days of plenty, when a boy or a man, coming to the lodge hungry from hunting or any other exertion, could eat right away. They remembered, too, the bad times of hunger when there was no food. But their people had never had rigid times to eat meals, unless they were moving camp and stopped to rest at a signal from the head men. They remembered feast and famine, both depending on whether food was available or scarce.

Even in the lean time before Stormy left the reservation, when there never was quite enough food, his mother had always pretended there was plenty and had never denied him or his father as long as anything was in the cooking pot, but the men exerted self-control and courtesy; they never ate as much as they wanted, because Stormy's mother and brother and sister must have some of whatever there was.

At the school, meals had to be eaten only at certain times, three a day, no matter how hungry a boy might be between times. At those times they ate prodigiously. At first, some of them ate too much and became sick. Other Lakotas tried to assure them that they need not stuff it all down, but they were required to speak English, which the established boys did not know well and the new ones did not know at all. If a boy used sign talk and was caught, the school disciplinarian cuffed him on the side of the head. This was a shocking thing to the Indian youths, who had never been struck in punishment by their own people, but they knew that was the way Wasichus acted toward children, even their own.

Having to sit at a table was strange to young people accustomed, as their ancestors had been, to sitting comfortably on the ground. Very slowly they learned to use forks. Sharp knives and spoons made of bone or horn had been all they needed at home.

The second-year or third-year pupils were not as helpful as they might have been to the newcomers. They had been through these miseries themselves and most of them felt superior now.

At the Carlisle Indian School, each new pupil was given a white man's name in front of his father's name, and it did not matter what his own name had been. So Stormy became Jack Elk Rising, and his friend Takes Much became William Scatters Them.

Receiving new names was no shock; all the older men they left behind them, and some of the women, had carried more than one name in their lifetimes. Every child began with a baby name; the great Sitting Bull had been called Slow as an infant, and Stormy's Grandmother Whirlwind had been They Love Her, because she was a much-wanted baby.

Stormy had received his name when his ears were pierced at the first Sun-gazing Dance after he was old enough to walk; the old warrior who gave it to him owned it, from a brave ancestor. The boy might have received a new name after he counted his first coup in battle in the old days, but there were no battles any more.

9

Paper That Talks

Stormy's parents did not see him for four years. Three years he was at the school, and part of another year he worked in a city, always sick for home. Each year, two pictures—one of the Lakota boys and one of the girls—came to the agency from the school. Elk Rising and Brings Horses and other relatives were allowed to look at them and study them.

The first one was the greatest shock, because they could not tell which of the boys was Stormy! All were dressed in uniforms; they looked grim and stern; none of them had long hair any more. Their braids had been cut off. Brings Horses sighed. Her boy had had pretty hair, long and thick and shining.

She picked out one face among dozens and said that was Stormy. Elk Rising commented, "They are suffering."

The same summer Stormy went away to school, in 1885, a big thing happened to Standing Tree. A Wasichu who called himself Buffalo Bill—the Indians called him Long Hair—was getting together a Wild West show to travel in the East, and his star attraction was to be Sitting Bull. There would be five other Lakota men, three women, and an interpreter. All of them would be paid money. Standing Tree was chosen as one of the men because he was very good-looking and a splendid rider. He felt embarrassed about wearing a costume that included an eagle-plume warbonnet, because he had never earned the right to wear one.

He traveled far, brought home money and many stories, but did not care to go away like that again.

He told his family and friends: "The chief is indeed a great man, with all the virtues, even patience before his enemies. All over where we went in the United States, people yelled at him and shook their fists, because Long Hair said he was the man who killed the big white chief at the Little Big Horn. But Sitting Bull paid no attention to that. He is a great chief, and he acted the way a great chief should, always dignified.

"Because the Wasichus hated him so much, they crowded to get in and see our show; they paid well for that. They crowded to buy the chief's picture, and he signed his name in English on the pictures and they paid him.

"When we traveled in the Grandmother's country, people crowded, too, but there they liked him, they showed him great respect."

Long Hair, Buffalo Bill, gave the chief two presents, a gray circus horse that could do tricks and a big white hat. These presents pleased Sitting Bull very much.

Two years later, Buffalo Bill planned to take his Wild West Show to England. Sitting Bull had been his great attraction before, and they had become friends, so Long

Hair asked him to come this time too. But the chief politely declined.

"My people need me here," he said. "The government is trying to take some more of our land away from us."

Long Hair was disappointed, but even without the chief his show was a great success in England. The people with him met Grandmother England herself, Queen Victoria, and she liked them.

But the chief's refusal got him into great trouble with McLaughlin the agent, because Mrs. McLaughlin, herself half Indian, had expected to go with the show as interpreter. But because the chief did not go, nobody from the agency could go. She was furious and spitefully urged her husband to watch Sitting Bull more closely than ever. Everything the old chief did irritated McLaughlin, anyway.

In spite of everything McLaughlin and others did to discredit him, Sitting Bull was and continued to be the Old Man Chief of the whole Sioux Nation.

There was no more serious pupil in the Carlisle school than Stormy—Jack Elk Rising. No matter how tedious the teaching, no matter how hard the learning, his attention never wavered. He listened, he imitated what was said in English. He used every English word he learned, no matter how stupid he felt about trying. When his teachers talked too fast, he did not become restless and give up. They noticed and were pleased with his progress. They took full credit for it.

The boys went to school in the morning and worked at white men's trades in the afternoon. The girls worked at housekeeping skills and sewing in the morning and had school in the afternoon.

There was one thing about Jack Elk Rising that did not please Captain Pratt at all: he rarely seemed to be having any fun. Pratt often had groups of important people visit the school—government men or church people who contributed money—and he was determined to show off his pupils. He trained them to play white boys' games with a ball, but only in their free time could they play the rough games of skill and strength that they had enjoyed back home. He had a white woman teach the girls exercises called calisthenics or physical culture. He himself taught the boys military drill, which they heartily hated. He even formed a band and had some of the more willing youths taught to play instruments that the church people bought. Captain Pratt showed off their obedience and discipline and tried to prove they were happy.

All this seemed to Stormy a stupid waste of time. He avoided all of it that he could. But he watched how the white people acted, wanting to know their idea of courtesy. And he listened to their talk.

His friend Takes Much was less enthusiastic about learning—more normal, Captain Pratt judged, even while reprimanding him for inattention. But Takes Much, William, learned some English, for the simple reason that if they were caught speaking Lakota or hand sign, they were both punished. They had to talk, because they were best friends, *kolas.*

If they had lived a generation earlier, they would have fought side by side in battle and risked their lives for each other. They would have slipped silently into camps of their enemies, the Crow Indians, to steal horses. In these new times, they helped each other when they could and suffered homesickness together but did not discuss it because there was no need. They simply endured spells of depression.

One day Takes Much, assigned to load garbage from the kitchen into a wagon, found an iron kettle that had a crack in it because someone had accidentally dropped it on stones outside the back door. He rescued the kettle and hid it, and when he had a chance, he said to Stormy in Lakota, "I found an iron pot. If we had a piece of hide, we could make a drum."

"Then we could sing!" Stormy agreed. He meant, and his friend understood, *Then we could pray properly. And Captain Pratt would not know what we were doing even when he heard us.*

The boys had all learned to be secretive, to talk briefly without being caught. After much secret whispering, Stormy found a Cheyenne youth who understood the hand-sign language and who had brought a big enough piece of buckskin from home. The Cheyenne had sore feet, because the heavy white man's shoes they all had to wear—shoes made in the school shop—did not fit him. He wanted to trade his buckskin for Stormy's extra pair of moccasins.

But that would not do, Stormy decided. They needed raw, untreated hide that would shrink and harden and pull the crack in the iron pot together. So they became scavengers and, at last, clever thieves. When two steers were slaughtered, they were watching for a chance at a hide. While Takes Much helped the slaughterhouse men with the second animal, Stormy cut a big enough piece of the raw, bloody hide of the first one to cover the top of the small kettle, with some hanging down around the edge.

Preparing it was harder than stealing it. The hide had to be kept wet in a hidden place and scraped clean on both sides. This was women's work that neither of them had ever paid much attention to—and they had to do it, and learn how to do it, in secrecy.

"Could we get a message to the older girls in their dormitory?" Takes Much wondered.

Stormy smiled. "You know we can't. Those precious flowers are too sacred for young men to approach. They can't read any better than we can write. And they probably don't know how to scrape a hide anyway."

The boys' mothers would have been shocked at the botch they made of it, scraping the wet hide clean when they could steal a few minutes at a time. They cut thongs from the scraps. They fastened the hide across the pot, tied it on tightly with the thongs, and let it dry. As the skin dried, it pulled the crack together, and they had their drum.

They made two drumsticks, padded with rags. The sound was not loud, but it was satisfactory. Captain Pratt frowned, because drumming and chanting were not things that white men did, but he did not punish the boys when they practiced. In fact, sometimes when visitors came to the school, he let the two youths put on a small exhibition of drumming and singing.

Visitors complimented the captain on what they called his "little Indian show," and he explained that this savagery was, of course, something the boys would outgrow as they became more civilized.

The other Lakotas, who understood perfectly what the songs meant, did not tattle. Sometimes two or three joined in with the chanted prayers to Wakan Tanka. But there was one song that Stormy always sang alone. The others recognized it as his; he had made it. The words were:

> The snake spirit looked at me, looked at me.
> The sky sent a voice with a message.
> It was cold on the hilltop.

To accompany this, his friend, his *kola,* used an unpadded drumstick skillfully to make a sound like a rattlesnake.

Stormy was one of the very few boys at the school who had gone on a vision quest, and he had honor among the others because of this.

On Sundays, all the pupils went to Sunday School in the town. Captain Pratt did not care which church any boy or girl went to; personally, he did not care whether they went at all, but the good will of the church people was important to him. Stormy and Takes Much tried all the churches and then settled down to the one where the Sunday school teacher of their age group spoke most slowly and repeated phrases most often. Stormy learned some English from him, although a great deal of it he could not understand at all. Because of his earnest listening to everyone who spoke English, he developed a permanent frown crease between his eyes, young as he was. Takes Much did not learn many new words in Sunday School or church. He usually went to sleep.

Writing and reading were taught in a very slow and tedious way in Pratt's school. Each pupil received a black slate and a peculiar pencil that would mark on it in white.

The marks could then be wiped off. A teacher made some marks on each boy's slate, then sent him away to figure out what to do with them. The more serious boys decided to copy these marks over and over. Others drew pictures of horses.

The marks were A B C D E F G, but nobody explained what they meant. Stormy copied until he could make marks almost like those the teacher had written.

After they went through other marks, ending with X Y Z—twenty-six altogether—which took several days, the teacher wrote on the blackboard with chalk: A B C, and said, "Ay, bee, see." The boys repeated. Thus they went clear through the alphabet but still had no idea what they were supposed to be learning or why. After many days some of them could look at one of those marks and pronounce it, but without any comprehension. The teacher did not know their language and they were being taught hers in the slowest, most tiresome way possible.

When the class began to work with numbers, a whole new world opened up. Numbers were magic. What could be done with them fascinated Stormy. Sometimes he caught the teacher making mistakes, but he was too wise to say anything.

The utter misery of homesickness struck all the pupils harder with the first signs of spring.

The girls' dormitory was too far from the boys' for the pupils to understand each other if they tried to shout back and forth, but they found a way to communicate. When sickness of the heart struck the girls and they longed for their homes and their relatives, they wailed in the old way of mourning, not sobbing privately and quietly as white girls might have done under the same circumstances.

The boys could hear that dismal wailing. They did their best to answer. They went to their windows, or outside when they were permitted, and sang the brave-up songs they had learned from their fathers and grandfathers, the same songs that had once given warriors courage when going into battle. That was the best they could do for the homesick girls.

Three boys ran away but did not get very far, because their uniforms were recognizable. Anyway, they had no money and no clear idea of how far away their homes were. Captain Pratt had them severely punished after they were caught and brought back.

Several of the younger girls became sick with longing for home and perhaps with more than that; two of them did not complain or tell the matron of their dormitory that they were sick—they simply died, a few days apart. Captain Pratt was very angry.

Stormy and his *kola*, Takes Much, found strength in chanting prayers to the Great Mystery while they beat the drum they had made.

What carried most of them through the last part of the winter was the promise of the "outing," as Pratt called his plan of sending them to work on farms for the summer. Any change was welcome, and so was the idea of living with families instead of in herds in the school dormitories.

From the beginning, Stormy had wanted to learn carpenter work in his half-days of shop at the school, because it might be useful in getting a job when he returned to the reservation. Instead, he had to learn shoemaking, which would be no use at all. He knew better than to argue; he was aware that Pratt was training Indians to live like whites, not to return to their homes with skills that would be useful on the reservation.

Sometimes when Stormy was especially depressed, he wondered: Did I misinterpret the meaning of the great echoing voice in my vision? *Help the people! Help the people!* Nobody could advise me then. There is nobody to advise me now. The school does not want me to help my people.

So he went on measuring and cutting leather to fit an iron last and pounding small nails to fasten on the soles.

One reason his people's moccasins were so comfortable, he thought, smiling, was that women made them with love as well as with skill. He was learning skill in making shoes, but he could never put any love into them.

Both Stormy and his *kola,* Takes Much, worked at shoemaking, so they could talk sometimes without being caught at it. One thing all the Indian pupils learned fast, because of the restrictions on language, was to be deceitful. The difficulty of having a friend made friendship more to be cherished. Stormy and Takes Much were very circumspect.

Stormy said quietly in Lakota, "Maybe we will learn something about how to farm well. My father is supposed to be a farmer, but he does not really know how."

"Mine too," his *kola* said. "I don't know what white farmers do. But I think the land here is better for growing crops, and there is much more rain."

Before telling the boys their assignments, the farmers for whom they would work, Captain Pratt lectured them about working hard, following orders, behaving politely, keeping clean, not getting into fights. He reminded them that they were lucky to have a chance to learn farming. (The girls, who went to work as household help, received a separate lecture.)

Captain Pratt felt that he knew each boy very well, because he watched them, or had them watched, closely, punished them for small infractions, and read the letters they wrote home, as well as the few letters that the lucky ones received from home.

So well had Stormy and Takes Much hidden their friendship that Pratt judged William Scatters Them to be an especially good boy, co-operative (he played baseball, marched fairly well in parades), obedient, and not much endangered by occasional savage singing and drumming.

But Jack Elk Rising he considered a serious problem —mostly because this one gave so little cause for complaint! And, of course, he was one of Sitting Bull's hostiles.

Pratt's criticism of Jack Elk Rising (carefully noted in a private file) was that this youth did not co-operate in activities. He did not willingly take part in white man's sports, except in foot racing; there he excelled. He was a good drummer, but did not care to learn the use of a drum in the band and was not good at marching. He was not enthusiastic about showing off for visitors. He did not complain. He was polite when he learned white man's politeness. He was not a lazy savage, as Pratt expected all Indians to be when they first came to the school. He did not match Pratt's idea of a normal Indian boy at all.

So it was hard for Pratt to decide where to send him

for the summer outing, and most of the boys were already placed on farms before the captain found a man who seemed suitable to take him in.

The man's name was Anderson; he was desperate for a farm hand, even one with no experience at all. Anderson said briefly that his hired hand had left without warning. He did not mention that this was his own son, age fifteen, who had run away from home, leaving a bitter, misspelled note saying he was never coming back. Anderson was a grim man who promised that he would indeed teach Jack Elk Rising more English, that he would provide comfortable sleeping quarters and plenty of food and a good Christian home. He had a wife and five little girls, the oldest being twelve.

Stormy found the farmer a constant scold, continually admonishing and correcting. Mrs. Anderson was a meek woman; she and the little girls were all afraid of her husband. He was very religious; he held family prayers and Bible reading every evening and prayed before meals while the food grew cold on the table. He prayed in anguish and spoke often of hellfire and the torments of sinners in eternity to come.

He impatiently taught his new helper to harness a team of work horses—animals bigger than any horses Stormy had ever seen before—and almost approved the way the youth handled them. Stormy had watched from a distance the way farm implements were used and tried to do exactly what Anderson said, but the farmer talked too fast and had no patience.

Stormy did not learn very much English; Mrs. Anderson and the little girls were afraid of him, and there was little time to talk because work was long, meals had to be eaten fast, and Stormy was sent out to the barn to sleep in the haymow right after evening prayers. He had never been lonelier except when he lamented to the spirits for his medicine.

He stayed with the Andersons two weeks. The farmer had brought him on a Sunday, and two Sundays later (after the family returned from church) the farmer undertook to convert him to his own religion. He said, "Boy, have you been baptized?"

Stormy replied, "No, sir." He understood something about what that meant, however.

Anderson gave him a sermon about what he must believe if he wanted to avoid damnation and eternal hellfire. "Are you ready for baptism, boy?" he demanded. "I can arrange it for next Sunday."

Stormy summoned up all his English and tried to explain that this was not what his people believed or what he believed. He wanted to explain about the Hereafter, about the Land of Many Lodges, and about all the spirits and the strength they gave. But he simply did not have enough English.

Anderson was shocked and angry. "Out!" he yelled. "You heathen, I won't have you around here! Get out! Go back where you came from!"

Stormy dodged to avoid a blow that Anderson aimed at his head.

In the barn, he hastily rolled up his small bundle of clothing. He walked out of the yard without looking back. He knew in which direction the school was. On the way to the farm in the wagon he had automatically noticed landmarks, such as groves of trees, farmhouses, big red barns, small bridges over streams.

In the bundle with his clothes were his heavy work shoes. He was more comfortable walking in moccasins, now much worn, that his mother had made with love. He did not know how far away the school was—he had had little experience in measuring by miles—but the wagon had taken four hours to cover the distance. He could walk almost as fast as the team had gone.

He gauged the time by the sun. It was a little after noon when he started his walk, without any dinner—which was a good meal on Sunday at the Anderson place, although cold after the farmer finished praying over the food.

He was very thirsty when, according to his calculations, he was about halfway back to the school. He saw a boy about his size pumping water in a farmyard and walked over to him, trying to think in English.

"Water," he said politely. "I have water?"

"Sure," the boy said, staring. "Hey, I bet you're one of the Injuns from the school." He handed Stormy a dipper full of water.

"Thank you," Stormy said. "Yes, school. I go school."

"Where you been?"

Jack had to think before he understood that. He answered, "Anderson farm. He say go." He gave back the dipper and was turning away when the boy yelled, "Pa! Hey, Pa! This Injun kid has been to Andersons' and I think the old sumbitch threw him out."

Stormy smiled. "Sumbitch" was one of the first English words he had learned from the soldiers at Fort Randall. It meant somebody you didn't like. He repeated, "Sumbitch," and the other boy laughed.

A man in clean overalls came out of the barn, a

red-faced, fattish man who smiled easily.

"What's wrong?" he inquired. "This lad got trouble?"

Stormy struggled to tell him. "I work Anderson. He want—want baptism me. Hellfire. Perdition. I say no. He say go."

The red-faced farmer frowned. "I'll bet he did, the old sumbitch." He stared keenly at Stormy. "You hungry?"

"Yes, sir. No eat."

"We'll fix that," the farmer promised. He bawled, "Martha! Heat up the chicken and dumplings! . . . Now you come on in the kitchen and we'll talk about this while you eat. Come on, Tom. You're always empty, too, even if you et two hours ago. What's your name, boy?"

"Jack Elk Rising, sir."

"I'm Joe Forman, and this is my boy Tom." They were walking fast toward the house. "Tell you what I'm going to do, Jack. I'll write a letter to Captain Pratt and tell him I want to hire you. Then you and my Tom can ride over to see him, and if he says yes, you come back here. How's that?"

When Stormy understood, he felt like whooping and yelling for joy. He grinned and replied, "Yes, *sir!*"

"But you eat first." They were at the kitchen door then. When "Jack Elk Rising" was introduced to the woman there, who was feeding wood into the kitchen stove to heat up the food, he said politely, "How do, ma'am." She was as nice as her husband and son.

He could hear music from a pump organ like the one they had at the school. It stopped and a girl older than Tom came out of another room.

The farmer smiled at her. "Bessie, got your old shoes on? Good. Catch up Ginger and Walt. I'll saddle 'em so the boys can ride over to Carlisle. This here's Jack Elk Rising."

Stormy stood up and said, "How do, ma'am," and was surprised when everybody thought there was something amusing about it. The girl went out and her father sat down to write a letter.

While the boys ate, he mumbled, wrote, and swore a little under his breath. Every time he did that, his wife said warningly, "Now, Joe! Not on Sunday!" but as if she liked him and felt it simply her duty to protest.

On the way to Carlisle, Stormy learned two English words, but Tom learned a dozen words of Lakota and several tricks about riding a horse. Stormy almost forgot how much afraid he was to face Captain Pratt and admit he was a failure at Anderson's farm.

Pratt was in no very good mood. When he finished reading the letter, his eyes blazed and he said, "Why, that sumbitch Anderson!" He paced the floor, muttering other words that Stormy had heard other soldiers use when they were angry. (Indian boys at the school were punished for using them.) Then Pratt said, "Of course you can go to Mr. Forman's. Tom, ask your father to come see me next time he drives to town."

That summer Stormy wrote his first letter home. He had not been able to write before, because his English was too limited and there was nobody to help him. The pupils at Carlisle were required to write home once a month after they were able, but they did not dare to say very much because Captain Pratt or one of the teachers censored the mail.

Now he had plenty of help. The Formans knew no Lakota, but the parents knew what any boy's parents would want to hear: that he was well and learning in school. He told his mother that he had a *kola* who knew her brother's family at Pine Ridge. The letter was rewritten several times, and Stormy copied it in his own handwriting. Mrs. Forman addressed it to Mr. and Mrs. Elk Rising, "care of Agent, Standing Rock Agency, Sioux Reservation, Dakota Territory." She also showed Jack, on a map in a book, where that was.

One thing he wanted to tell his parents was that the school had taken away his medicine bag, but he did not know the English for that, so he used the Lakota word, writing it the way it sounded. He said he had lost it, and he knew they would understand. He still had the seven-button rattle from the snake he had killed, though. That was easy to hide.

The writing and sending of the letter was a triumph for the whole household. Stormy learned an important thing: that there could be family love among the Wasichus as there was among his own people. He had not noticed any in all the time he had been gone.

He worked hard and learned much that summer.

His parents had to have the postmaster at the agency read the letter for them; they were joyful and proud, but they could not answer because the postmaster was too busy and any interpreter who could have done it would require payment. They could not pay.

When the summer outing ended, Stormy was able to help Takes Much write in English to his parents at Pine Ridge, and thereafter both boys wrote home proudly, although with great difficulty and many errors, once a month, in spite of the poor methods of teaching English at the school.

At Pine Ridge, Scatters Them and his wife and their three children memorized every word of the Lakota translation of Takes Much's letter, and Morning Rider and his family learned every word of it from them, jubilant that now they had a tie with their relatives at Standing Rock. And at Grand River, Stormy's parents memorized the Lakota translations of their educated boy's letters, warmed with happiness at knowing that he had an Oglala *kola* who knew their Pine Ridge relatives.

Sitting Bull himself expressed profound satisfaction with the progress of Stormy, whom the white men called Jack Elk Rising.

10

Whispers of Paradise

After two years, Stormy was accustomed to being called Jack Elk Rising. He had had two summer "outings" at the Forman farm, had improved his English greatly, and had learned something about carpentry, because he helped Mr. Forman and his son to build a new barn. At the school, however, Captain Pratt still refused to let him learn that trade. Instead he had to work at tinsmithing, for which there was no use at all back home. He looked forward to a third summer with the Formans, but Captain Pratt assigned him to a different farm in spite of Mr. Forman's protests.

"Jack needs diversity in experience," Pratt said sternly. "I'm assigning him to a different farm. I'll get you another good boy."

"Don't get me any boy," Forman growled, "if I can't have that one!"

So Stormy went obediently—what else could he do?— to the Winslow place, where the people seemed half afraid of him, and wholly suspicious, because he was a Sioux Indian. He heard Mrs. Winslow's nervous, hysterical mother cry, "We'll all be murdered in our beds!"

Here he slept in a shed and ate his meals after the family did. But at least he had company for meals, a girl called Rose Running Deer, a Cherokee from Carlisle School. She helped in the kitchen and worked hard around the house. They spoke English together. Mrs. Winslow, with an idea that they were not good enough to eat with the family, did not trust them together, so she usually watched them eat, scowling and listening and urging them to hurry up.

Stormy pitied the girl. Several times he found her crying while she loaded stovewood on her arm to carry into the house. He tried to comfort her, but it was no use.

With some romantic idea of rescuing her, he said one day, "If you want to run away, maybe I could help you, take you to my people."

She set her mouth in a stubborn line. "I am not going to live like an Indian. I am going to marry a white man and live civilized."

Stormy felt as if he had been slapped. "Good luck to you, Rose," he answered. "Some day I will go home and marry a girl of my people."

That was his last outing. He had a talk with Captain Pratt at the end of summer; Takes Much was there too. Both young men wanted the same thing: to stop school and go home.

"The agreement was three years, sir," Stormy reminded Pratt. "Now we are finished."

"The rules have changed," Pratt said brusquely. "Now pupils stay five years if they want to graduate."

"I finished three years," Stormy insisted.

"So did I," his *kola* said. "Now I want to quit school."

Somehow—they were never quite sure how he did it—Pratt persuaded them that, although they could cease going to school now, they should try for a while living like civilized people, earning their own living. He would find them jobs in Harrisburg, making shoes; they were both trained for that.

"Live like white men do," he urged. "Pay your own way, don't depend on the government." (They knew they were being insulted, but they had learned to hold their tempers.) "Live in a boardinghouse like other single working men, go to church, be independent. You will enjoy it."

Stormy longed to get back home to the reservation. But he remembered what Sitting Bull had said about having an interpreter he could trust. Perhaps he could be of more use to the chief if he followed Pratt's advice and tried the experience of living like a white man for a while.

So the two young men agreed to go to Harrisburg, but they didn't enjoy it. Pratt did find them jobs together in a shoe factory, at low wages because they were beginners, and he found them a place to live and eat their meals with other single men. Before he sent them out into the world, he gave them a lecture; he was good at giving lectures.

"Go to church," he advised. "It is a way to meet other people so you will have friends. Get acquainted with the men at your rooming house. But be careful of bad women! They will come up to you on the street and ask you to their rooms, and you have to pay them. But they will give you a bad disease. Maybe they will rob you of your money, too. Stay away from them!"

The two young men said respectfully, "Yes, sir," with

their Sioux faces as solemn as if they were in council with great chiefs.

"Stay away from liquor," Pratt advised sternly. "Indians can't stand liquor. They lose their wits. I don't want you to end up in jail. Don't drink strong spirits!"

Both young men said, "We won't, sir," and meant it.

Afterward, in private, they laughed harder than Pratt would have suspected Indians could laugh, and kept repeating, "Bad women! No sir, yes sir."

They knew more about bad women than the school authorities dreamed they knew. That was a subject of great interest and much secret conversation in the dormitory. Hired men on farms where they had worked talked about bad women all the time, whether they had any experience or not. The farmers for whom they worked had solemnly warned them about bad women.

Stormy and Takes Much told each other, but not outsiders, white men, what had happened to bad women among their own people a generation or two earlier; these stories were handed down. But those things happened in the old days, the clean days, when the Lakotas followed their own rigid laws or terribly punished those who broke them. Stormy remembered the story of a distant relative of his who had bitten the knife to swear it was true that he and a certain married woman had committed adultery. The man was not punished, but the woman's husband cut her nose off and she went out in the woods and hanged herself.

Around the agencies, too, there were bad women, some white, some Indian, now that the white man ruled their lives. Stormy and Takes Much even knew how to identify a bad woman in Harrisburg, although they had not been there to see one: "They wear war paint, as our fathers and grandfathers used to; that's how you tell."

As for whiskey, strong spirits, they knew about that too. Stormy remembered the old story about a relative of his named Pemmican Woman who had suffered greatly because her husband went wild from whiskey when they lived down near Fort Laramie.

"I think it is true that Indians can't stand liquor," Takes Much said.

"Neither can a lot of white men," Stormy agreed.

"Will you go to church?" Takes Much inquired, smiling with one side of his mouth.

"Never," Stormy answered. "The whites lie to themselves. They say they will act good, but they act bad. I do not want to go to their heaven. That man I worked for once, the farmer Anderson, might be there. I want to go to the Land of Many Lodges where my people are and everything is the way it used to be."

They worked at their jobs, shared a bleak room, found that other men at the boardinghouse either looked down at them or seemed afraid. And everything was too much indoors.

They walked a great deal on Sundays, glad to be away from the machines and workbenches in the factory, needing to exercise their bodies. But they walked on sidewalks, not on the earth. Even in public parks, where there were trees and bushes and grass, they did not feel close to the earth.

They had no friends but each other. People avoided them. They were an island among thousands of strangers.

Stormy wrote a letter home once a month, sounding

cheerful, not daring to write oftener; those back home who could translate the English into Lakota would lose patience with his father if asked too often. Twice his father had a letter written, telling in careful, guarded terms about troubles on the reservation. Stormy and Takes Much had already heard rumors from new boys before they left the school, but the rumors were confusing. Something about threats of the government to take away a great deal of the Sioux Reservation lands.

Takes Much had said with regret, "I wish we were allowed to tell many things to them. We could help them, but they have to learn hard, the same as we did."

"We learned to be"—Stormy had searched for an English word—"to be sly. In three years we learned that." He laughed, briefly and bitterly.

Tuesday, January 1, 1889, was a school holiday at Carlisle because it began the white man's New Year. There were no classes (*washtay!* good) and there was an extra good dinner *(washtay)!* There was an extra long prayer before the dinner by a visiting Catholic priest and a longer one after it by an Episcopalian. (Not so good, but the pupils knew how to behave.) Altogether, a pretty good day.

In Harrisburg, Stormy and Takes Much had the day off but nothing to do, no place to go. They talked about home and drank a small bottle of whiskey they had bought, because all the other men in the rooming house were doing the same thing. Takes Much had to cough often. Stormy's head felt stuffed up with a cold. It was not a good day.

On that day, in a faraway state that the whites called Nevada, which few if any of the pupils at Carlisle had ever heard of, a strange thing began to happen that would change the lives of most Indians and end the lives of many. The sun slowly died. The Indians there, the Paiutes, peaceful, long conquered, became frantic. They shouted and wailed and fired off guns to frighten away whatever supernatural monster had swallowed the sun and made the daytime dim. They were successful, and slowly the monster disgorged the sun so that it shone again. Another terrible peril had been overcome.

One Paiute man, a young man with prophetic powers, had been suffering from a fever. His name was Wovoka, and because he worked for a white farm family named Wilson, he was also known as Jack Wilson. He had considerable spirit power, including five songs to control the weather. The day the sun died, so did Wovoka.

But he did not seem truly dead. If his skin was cut with a knife, it still bled. After a few days Wovoka opened his eyes, and the people rejoiced, especially his loyal wife Mary, who had grieved bitterly.

Someone kneeling by him asked, "Where were you?"

Wovoka sat up and replied, "With God."

Then he told them of the wonders of the place where he had been. It was a pleasant land, full of game. All the Indian people who had ever lived were there, busy as they used to be busy, all happy.

"God told me to come back," he said. "And I must tell the people to be good and love one another, not to quarrel, but to live in peace with the whites. Our people must work and not lie or steal. They must put away war. And then we will all be reunited with our loved ones who are dead. There will be no more sickness or death or old age.

"I have brought you a dance, with the songs and prayers that go with it. Perform this dance when I tell you, for five days at a time, and after a while all the spirits of the dead and the pony herds and the buffalo will come back and we will all be happy."

Wovoka did not claim to be the son of God, but many of his followers believed he was the Messiah, and spoke of him as Christ. He preached peace and friendship and hope. But he was to set the West on fire with the promise of the Dance of Spirits Returning, which the whites called the Ghost Dance because they feared it and did not understand it.

Neither did some of Wovoka's most ardent and earnest apostles understand his teachings. That was why the dance set the West on fire, especially among the Sioux, who were suffering the most.

*   *   *

On a day in spring, sitting huddled on a bench in a public plot of open space in Harrisburg, the two young men were cold but at least they were in the open air. It smelled better than the air in their boardinghouse.

"Winter has gone. One more winter. But this is not like early spring back home," Takes Much mused. He shuffled his heavy white-men's shoes in the dirt.

Stormy agreed. "This earth is not our mother. Too many human feet have sucked the life from it." He added in English, "To hell with civilization!"

Takes Much nodded agreement. "Civilized is not to have relatives, not to trust anybody."

They were silent together, not needing to talk. Stormy had learned all he could at school, but his English was "Injun English." He understood the language pretty well, but putting the words together to talk it was harder.

132

Was this any way to help the people? Nothing he did in Pennsylvania helped his people in Dakota, except that he sent home money when he had some to spare. He did not waste any money.

"Tomorrow we go to work," he said, and they wandered back to their boardinghouse, where white men looked at them strangely and avoided them.

The men in the shoe factory were working at their machines and benches when the boss called Stormy into his cluttered cubbyhole of an office. He was scowling. He stared at him for a while before speaking. Then he said, "Copy them invoices for me on them forms, just like they are, and add them up."

Stormy did so in his best handwriting; adding the dollars and cents was easy. The boss checked every one, then said, "You write a fair hand, and you can add. Now I'm of a mind to promote you, with a little raise. My clerk says he's quitting. You want the job?"

That was not really a question, any more than asking a hungry dog if it wanted meat. Stormy said, "Yes, sir. I can do it."

"OK, go back to work. You start the new job next Monday—anyhow I'll give you a chance to prove yourself."

Stormy said with dignity, "Thank you, sir," and walked out.

The boss called Takes Much into his office next and spoke roughly.

"I've had too many complaints about you," he said. "The other men don't like having you here because you're sick. You cough. They're afraid you got consumption and they'll get it from you. I can't take no chances on that. Tough luck, but you got to go. I'll pay you off now, through today, even if you ain't earned all that."

He handed over an envelope with money already counted in it.

"This place not healthy to work," Takes Much said brusquely. "Air bad."

"It's healthy enough if sick men stay out of it," growled the boss. "What you waiting for? You're all through here."

Takes Much with his bad news walked to the bench where Stormy worked with his good news. Both were smiling.

"I am leaving tomorrow," Takes Much said gently. "Going home. He says I am sick with consumption, and I think he is right. I have thought so for a long time."

Stormy stood up, cold with anger. "Just wait a minute."

He walked into the boss' office and said, in English, "You are no man. You stink like a dog long time dead. Now I will tell you so you never forget!"

Standing there in the doorway, he raged in the Lakota language. He sang and chanted. He repeated himself in the hand sign. He compared the boss to every vile thing he could think of, his voice rising and falling hypnotically.

The boss was so terrified that he began to yell, "Help! Get the police!"

None of the workmen moved. Those who were not almost paralyzed with fear at this unheard-of savage ritual were, in fact, enjoying it, because they detested the frightened little man, ordinarily so pompous, who was the center of it.

One workman did move two steps toward the front door, but his way was blocked by Takes Much, who was not saying a word. He was simply standing there, scowling, a very tall Sioux Indian, and silently talking in hand sign, with menacing gestures. (He was telling how he had conquered many enemies in many battles. He had never been in any battle, but what difference did that make?)

Takes Much and Stormy walked out together and never looked back. The boss collapsed and had to be revived with brandy. Nobody told the police. The boss was sure he would drop dead of the Indian curse if he did.

The two Lakotas walked the eighteen miles from Harrisburg to Carlisle, found Captain Pratt, and courteously but firmly demanded that he pay them enough money to take them back to Dakota.

Pratt set his jaw and argued: "You didn't stay five years," he reminded them. "We are not obliged to pay your return fare because you dropped out of school after three years."

Stormy set *his* jaw. "You changed rule after we got here. That is how white men deal with Indians in treaties."

Pratt turned red with fury. "How dare you talk to me that way!"

"Because I am a man," Stormy told him. "And a Lakota." Some of his English left his mind under stress. "Because my *kola* sick. Maybe die. He want to go home before he die."

That word "consumption," which their boss had used, was well and terribly known to them. Takes Much *was* sick; he had been coughing for a long time.

Captain Pratt calmed down. He became concerned (Indians were susceptible to consumption, he well knew). He called a doctor from town, sending a letter by a white man on a horse.

The doctor examined Takes Much, and it was true. He did have consumption. The doctor recommended plenty of fresh air and good food. Back home there was fresh air. Food depended on the whim of the government and the honesty of the agent.

Pratt gave them enough money to get home and even wrote out instructions for getting there. He shook hands with both of them and said, "Good luck, boys."

"We are not boys," Stormy replied briefly. "We are men."

And so they left. Takes Much remarked in Lakota, "As you said, they taught us to be sly, and that promises are made to be broken. But we knew that."

He laughed shortly. Then he coughed.

PART IV

THE
MESSIAH IS ON EARTH

1889

11

Faith Is Lost

When they set out for home, Stormy and Takes Much were still not quite sure how Takes Much was going to get to Pine Ridge. The two could travel together across the country by train, then—still together—on a steamboat up the Missouri, but Pine Ridge was very far from the river and there were two ways to get there.

A railroad ran through northern Nebraska, along the southern border of the Rosebud and the Pine Ridge reservations. Takes Much could leave the steamboat and ride on that railroad to a little town named Thacher. Then he would be 130 miles from Pine Ridge Agency. Or he could stay on the boat longer, get off at Rosebud Landing, which the Lakotas called Black Pole, and he would be 190 miles from home. Either way, he could hitch a ride on a freight wagon for several days of travel.

"I think I can," he said, smiling. "If the driver is Indian, he may refuse me because of my Wasichu clothes. If he is a Wasichu, he may refuse me because I am an Indian. No, really, there will be no trouble. I think I will go on to Black Pole, to ride longer on the fireboat with you."

There was plenty of time to talk on the long, long journey home from Pennsylvania. Nobody cared whether they spoke together in English or Lakota or hand sign. White men stared at them anyway, some with hatred, so sometimes the two friends spoke Carlisle English—Injun English—together just to prove they could. But in talking of important matters, they used Lakota.

Stormy told again of the great echo and the command from the sky: *Help the people! Help the people!* He told of the snake with the forked, flickering tongue, the snake that looked at him and passed him by but hurt someone else whom he could not see and did not know.

"So after a while I offered to go to Carlisle," he concluded. "It seemed like the only way to help the people. But that is not what Carlisle is for."

"No, it is not," Takes Much agreed. "I went because my father thought it would be good." He reflected. "The forked tongue, the sign for white man. The snake, danger, but not to you." He shivered.

Knowing his thought, Stormy murmured, "The danger was to you. We had not even met."

Takes Much smiled a little. "I think I am going to die of the consumption. People die of it at home, too. Everyone dies, my friend. Nothing endures but the earth. I will be at home among my people, who love me.

"Sometime I'll see you again. In the Land of Many Lodges. We will kill buffalo together. We will fight enemies side by side. We will walk in honor, like our grandfathers. Our women will pitch our lodges close."

They sat on the dusty green seat of the train, not

glancing at each other, grieving but tearless.

Making a hard little joke, Stormy said, "If the Christian church songs are right, we will fly around their heaven, singing."

"If that is what they want, let them do it," Takes Much replied. "I want to wear feathers in my hair and ride a good spotted pony."

The farther west they traveled, the more the whites avoided them, seemed to detest them, went out of their way to be insulting. Four years earlier, the youngsters heading for Carlisle had been stared at and laughed at because of the way they were dressed and the way they acted. Now they dressed like white men, behaved like white men—but the whites hated them.

Takes Much murmured, "They are pushing in more and more. They want *all* our land."

"They want to push us off the earth," Stormy agreed.

When it came time to board the steamboat, they noticed that a pompous official looked at the tickets of passengers who boarded ahead of them, counted the people the tickets included, and had the passengers write their names in a book, with their destinations in a separate column. Then he returned the ticket in each case.

When Stormy's turn came, the official looked at him, then at the ticket.

"Write your name here," he growled. "Or can you write?"

"I can write," Stormy replied quietly. He wrote his name, Jack Elk Rising, and destination, Fort Yates.

"All right, go on," the official ordered.

"Give me my ticket," Stormy told him.

The man hesitated, then gave it to him in a surly way.

Stormy guessed that his intention had been to put him off the boat before it reached Fort Yates, just for spite, because without the ticket he could not prove that he had paid to go that far.

Takes Much followed his example about getting back his ticket.

"You eat with the Injuns and sleep on the deck," the surly man ordered.

The young men nodded. Everyone who paid only the minimum fare slept on the deck, and they preferred to associate with their own people anyway, although the food would be even worse than what the white deck passengers got. They were among enemies. But they were going home!

The following day, they were leaning on the railing, smelling the clean air, smelling spring, as the steamboat struggled slowly against the current, when a little white boy ran up and stared. The child's father, dressed like a farmer, leaped to snatch the boy away, scolding, "Stay away from them savages! They might scalp you!"

Stormy pretended not to understand. He took off his hat and said in Lakota, in a polite tone of voice, "I would not dirty my father's lodge with the lousy scalp of one of your family. You are the son of a she dog and I spit on you."

An old man with a tobacco-stained white beard and well-worn clothing barked with laughter and said in English, "Go it, boy. I think the same."

Stormy was startled. He replied in Lakota, "I thought nobody would understand the language of my people."

In the same tongue, the old man said, "I had a Sans Arc girl for a wife when I was your age, and a Brulé woman after that. Later on I had a white one, but she was no good at keeping a man happy and comfortable."

Stormy tried to comfort him. "They will be waiting for you in the Land of Many Lodges, grandfather."

The old man barked laughter again. He said, in English this time, "Not the white one. If the Lord is merciful, she's gone to her idea of heaven, and that's a hell of a long ways off from mine."

He was going to the same landing as Takes Much, and then to the Pine Ridge Agency. "We'll have no trouble catching a ride," he promised. "I still got friends."

Stormy and Takes Much enjoyed his company.

"You fellows will have to relearn your manners," he reminded them. "You stare me straight in the face when you're talking. Do you do that with old men when you're home?"

"No, grandfather," Takes Much agreed in Lakota. "Captain Pratt made us do that, like soldiers. But among our people, it is rude."

So they practiced the old way, the good way, on the steamboat, of not looking straight at the person they were talking to—and the whites thought they were tricky and evasive.

When Stormy and Takes Much parted, they embraced like Lakotas, shook hands like white men, and wanted to cry like women.

During the rest of the steamboat journey, Stormy passed the time getting used to his own country. There were many passengers. If a white man spoke to him, Stormy answered in his best English, looking him straight in the face and giving his name, if asked, as "Jack Elk Rising from the Carlisle Indian School." If an old-man Indian spoke, Stormy answered in Lakota, with eyes cast down, saying, "I am called Stormy, son of Elk Rising of the Hunkpapas. I am going home to Grand River."

Sometimes he thought, I am one man with two faces, and it will not be easy to keep track of myself. And I have two names at one time. Who am I? Does anyone care?

He cared, because in spite of all the misery, he had not yet done anything to help the people and did not know what he could do.

Stormy's family did not know he was coming. They lived forty miles from the agency and went to it only for ration days, with team and wagon, pitching the lodge there with other lodges.

He ran down the gangplank at Fort Yates and began to walk toward the agency, greeting people he knew. This *was* ration day. As he neared the agency, a young Lakota told him where to find his father's lodge, and he walked straight to it, smiling.

His mother, Brings Horses Woman, looked up at him over an armful of firewood, gasped, and then screamed. She dropped the wood and ran to him. He dropped his suitcase and his bundle and gathered her into his arms.

He forgot he was a grown man. He hugged her as a little boy hugs his mother when he needs comfort. Now he was over six feet tall and she looked small before him; he could feel her bones—she was very thin.

She screamed, "Elk Rising! Saved Her Cub! Come!" Then she made the trilling sound that women used to greet returning men whom they wished to honor for courage and success.

In a moment, Stormy's father and brother-shadow

were there. Elk Rising embraced him without words. The boy, Saved Her Cub, sixteen now and big, hung back respectfully, then held out his right hand like a white man. Stormy gripped it, then embraced him, hands on shoulders, in the old way, smiling and close to tears.

Elk Rising said, "There is your bed place. Your mother always keeps it ready. It has always been ready since you went away."

"And my sister, Red Pipe Girl? She has seventeen winters now and is a woman."

She had not come in the wagon this time, they said. He would see her as soon as they got home to Grand River.

That was all the family there was now. White Mountain was a farmer and married. He had wanted to become a medicine priest, but that was forbidden. Standing Tree, also married, was still very loyal to Sitting Bull and had his lodge near the chief's cabin. He had driven the chief up to the agency just the day before on a strange errand —to meet a white woman!—and he would come to tell them what had happened. Why should the great Sitting Bull trouble himself to meet a strange white woman? It was hard to believe.

Brings Horses apologized, "There is nothing to eat yet, Son, because they have not distributed the rations. It should have started this morning."

So close they lived to starvation! "I have saved some money to buy treats," Stormy told her. "And I want to look over the trader's store anyway. My father and brother and I will walk over there now."

He wanted to look over all the activities at the agency, to see what hope there might be for a job there. He had noticed no building going on at the fort and had learned that when there was any carpenter work to be done, the soldiers did it.

At the trader's store there were few customers. A surly clerk ignored Elk Rising but stared at Stormy in his white man's working clothes. Stormy jingled some coins in his pocket, and the owner of the store bustled up to do business with this Indian who had money. Stormy looked around and took his time, showing off his English to ask prices—they were very high—pretending he had all the money in the world to spend. He consulted his father about what food would be a treat, not included in the rations. Nothing in the garden was big enough to harvest, Elk Rising told him, and they always hungered for fruit.

He bought canned peaches and some apples and potatoes and onions, writing down in his notebook the price of each thing as it was placed on the scarred wooden counter—partly to hint to the trader that he would be hard to cheat, partly to let the man know he could write. The trader scowled. Stormy asked his father, "There will be no meat until tomorrow when the rations are given?" and bought a piece of corned beef so there would be a good stew in the pot. He added some hard candy that everybody liked.

When he had what he wanted, the trader said, "Five dollars and twenty cents," and held out his hand. Stormy said politely, "I owe four dollars and twenty cents. See, I have added up everything," and showed him the notebook.

The trader was plainly angry that he could not cheat this customer, but he was impressed, too. He went over the figures carefully, adding slowly, and finally agreed,

"Yeah, you're right. I see where the mistake in adding was." Stormy paid him.

Stormy did not think that was a place where he wanted to work, but he had laid the foundation if he had to come back there and ask for a job.

"I ain't seen you around here before," the trader remarked.

Stormy replied, "My name is Jack Elk Rising. This is my father, Elk Rising. I went to Carlisle Indian School three years. Then I worked in Harrisburg, Pennsylvania. Now I am home."

His father wrapped the purchases in his blanket, except the corned beef; Saved Her Cub carried that on the end of a sharpened stick and had to fight off hungry dogs all the way back to their canvas lodge. He swore at them fluently in English; that was about all the English he knew, although he had attended the government's new day school at the agency for a while.

Supper was late, because the meat took a long time to cook for the stew, but it was a fine supper. Brings Horses was entranced by the canned peaches—such extravagance! She was ladling stew into their bowls when Standing Tree arrived, astonished and delighted to see Stormy. They embraced in the Lakota way.

Standing Tree exclaimed, "You are a man! You look like a white man almost."

"But I am a Lakota man of the Hunkpapas. I am Stormy, son of Elk Rising and Brings Horses Woman. I am home now."

"Tell us about all the time you were gone, and what you will do now."

Stormy answered without flinching: "They were not

good years, but I learned some things. I learned not to trust white men. Now I will go to Grand River for a while. Then maybe I will come back to the agency and try to get a job that pays money."

His mother moaned. "But you will come home sometimes?"

"Of course he will," Stormy's father answered for him.

Stormy said, "Tell us about the white-woman stranger. The rest of my story can wait."

Standing Tree chuckled. "She has been writing him letters from back East. She belongs to some club that she calls the National Indian Defense Association. She is rich and wants to help the chief in his fight to keep the government from taking more reservation land away for the white men. She had a big fight with White Hair, the agent —he had opened and read her letters before the chief received them, so he knew who she was.

"No, I will not eat, thank you. The white woman took us to the boardinghouse and paid for it all. The wife of Sitting Bull would not go in there—she said she would rather be hungry, because she would not know how to act. The white lady piled up a plate of food and took it out to the wagon for her—think of that! A rich white woman waiting on a Lakota woman!"

His listeners put their right hands over their mouths in token of astonishment.

"The white woman came to paint a picture of the chief; she says he is a great man. Of course he is, but White Hair the agent is angry when anyone says so. She wants him to go to the lower agencies, with her along, to talk to the chiefs down there and persuade them not to sign the government's papers to give away more Indian land.

But he cannot go without a pass from the agent, and I think White Hair will not give a pass. That is what they were fighting about."

Stormy's heart was on the ground. How was he going to help the people if Sitting Bull had somebody else reading and translating his letters for him? And this rich white woman, who dared to fight with the agent, could do more for the chief than Stormy could.

"But how did she *talk* to Sitting Bull?" he asked.

"She hired an interpreter, a half-blood Lakota. Maybe he would lie to *her,* but he would not dare try to fool the chief. She has money to throw around! She wants to live at Grand River to help him. She wants to learn Lakota. But she cannot stay on the reservation without the agent's permission, and she has made him very angry."

Standing Tree was full of excitement about the fight and amusement about the rich white woman. He went on:

"The woman wrote to the chief last summer. She sent him maps and warned him about just what the commission from Washington was doing and what the land was worth that they wanted to take away from us. Sitting Bull is strong; he says 'No,' but other chiefs are weak or confused. They give in, get scared, they say 'Yes, yes.' Especially," Standing Tree added grimly, "when the agents say they will cut our food rations even more and take away even more of our clothing annuities that were promised long ago by treaty."

Stormy's father murmured, "Already some of our people are starving. We die; especially the children sicken and die. We eat beef and fry-bread—but there is never enough."

"The white woman is kind," Standing Tree explained. "She does not want us cheated."

Stormy had another question: "How was the chief able to read her letters?" (Have I wasted four years, he wondered, when I thought I could help my people? Sitting Bull does not need me!)

"I took them to interpreters who could read and write," Standing Tree explained. "Never the same one twice. They told me what was said on the paper-that-talks, and I put it here"—he pointed to his head— "and went back and told the chief. He did not need to answer. The woman says she is going to do something, and she does it."

After they went home in the wagon with their rations, they used up most of the food in a feast to which they invited many people to celebrate Stormy's homecoming. Stormy met his sister—a sullen girl, rather bold, who had forgotten to carry enough water to their little garden, had forgotten to do about everything she was supposed to do. Stormy felt like scolding her but did not do so, realizing that she expected it and was looking for a reason to argue with him.

She asked in a challenging way, "What did you learn in all this time?"

"All I could," he answered, and turned his back.

He was flattered, almost comforted, by a visit from Sitting Bull himself as soon as the latter came back from the agency. The chief rode a fine gray horse that Buffalo Bill, Long Hair, had given him. He honored Stormy by dismounting before he shook hands. Then he embraced the young man and, holding him by the shoulders, looked up into his face. The chief was not a tall man.

"Have you found the meaning of your vision?" he asked.

"I have not found it," Stormy answered.

"You suffered," Sitting Bull said. "The scars are on your heart. But you endured. And you must have learned something."

"I learned some things. We all had to endure."

"Did you adopt the white man's religion?"

"I said their prayers and sang their songs, because these things were required. But I do not believe."

"What did you gain?"

"Knowledge, a little, and how to hate. I do not want to be civilized."

"Nothing about your vision?"

Stormy told him sadly about the snake of consumption that had passed him by but was killing his *kola*.

Just then Red Pipe Woman and her girl friend came around the corner of the cabin and, seeing the two men, stared boldly and switched the fringes of their shawls.

"Go in the lodge," Stormy commanded sharply. "Women do not interrupt when men are talking." The girls scurried away.

Sitting Bull asked, "Will you go out to dream again?"

Stormy was startled by the question, but he was a man of the Lakotas and did not betray that emotion. He replied, "Maybe."

"We used to do that," the chief said. "It refreshes a man's spirit."

Stormy remembered that Sitting Bull had lamented many times.

The chief added, "But I would not advise any man

about a thing like that. It is private, for him alone to decide."

"If there is anything I can do for the people, I will do it," Stormy offered.

This was the time for the chief to say, *You can read and write for me,* but he did not. He said only, "Yes," and turned away.

Stormy shuddered at the misery he saw all around him. Fry-bread and tough beef, those were the staples of diet, and they always ran out before ration day. Children were sickly. Old people did not survive illness. Rations had been cut, and the annuity of clothing and blankets. Nobody knew whose fault it was. Agent McLaughlin had his Metal Breasts explain (when anyone would listen) that it was not his fault; the Grandfather in Washington had simply not sent enough of anything, and that was the fault of something called Congress. Stormy had an idea what Congress was—a bunch of white men who did not care what happened to Indians now that they had surrendered—but what was there to do about it? Nothing.

His heart was lifted by the fact that he could communicate with his *kola* by letters. He had little good news to tell and did not wish to burden Takes Much with any other kind. He wrote a letter for his mother, Brings Horses, to her brother at Pine Ridge. They had been apart now for eight years. He sent it to Takes Much to translate for them.

Brings Horses told Morning Rider, her brother, that their family was small now—her husband, Elk Rising; Stormy, their oldest son, had been to school at Carlisle but was home; their second son, Saved Her Cub, was a fine big boy; Red Pipe Girl, their daughter, was a woman; White Mountain and Standing Tree were married and had their own homes. She did not need to mention those long dead: Blue Rock Woman, who had been wife to Elk Rising, or Wakan Woman, the pitiful Nez Percé. She did not mention that Saved Her Cub was not their born-to-them son but a Nez Percé. Her brother and his family would remember.

The family gathered around and watched with admiration while Stormy wrote the letter in English and his mother made her X beside her name. She even wrote her name in pictures: a stick-figure woman leading three stick horses. They would mail the letter from the agency next ration day.

Saved Her Cub, watching Stormy write, resolved to try going to school again—if they did not cut his hair. There was a government school now at Grand River, badly taught. Both he and Red Pipe Girl had for a while attended a boarding school at Standing Rock Agency, forced to enroll because Agent McLaughlin cut off the rations of entire families until the school filled its quota. Hunger had made them pupils, but nothing made them enthusiastic. Saved Her Cub's braids had been cut off at school; now his hair was long enough to make stubby braids, and he was not going to go through that any more, school or no school. Red Pipe Girl had not learned anything but sullenness and what it was to be homesick.

Next day Stormy told his mother he was going somewhere to be by himself. He walked for two hours away from the village, trying to feel at home under the sky, on the earth, but feeling like a stranger here. He heard birds and watched them, but they meant nothing. Insects flew or crawled and he watched, but they were only insects. He cried out, "Wakan Tanka!" and there was no sign.

He stripped himself naked and shouted again, "Wakan Tanka!"

Then he stooped to the little pile of his clothing and took the knife from his belt sheath. He stood again, stared at the sun, and cried, "All the spirits, I offer my blood!"

High on his left leg, where the scars would not normally show, he made a gash, and another and another. The blood ran down. Three gashes—but three was the Christians' sacred number. He cut again, to make the Lakotas' sacred number: four.

There was no uplift for his own spirit, no sign from anywhere. He was only a naked man under the sky with blood running down his leg and a knife in his hand.

He screamed to the sun. Nothing happened.

He stood there trembling with the shock of a realization he had been trying to avoid: *I do not believe any more! I have lost my faith in Wakan Tanka. I have lost everything I had!*

He lay down on the rough earth, naked, letting sharp weeds and pebbles bite into his back, feeling the hot sun on his skin, and waited until the gashes stopped bleeding. He made a pad of weeds and tied it over the cuts so that if they opened he would not get blood on his pants and have to explain it to his mother when she washed his clothes. He dressed and walked back to the village.

He had lost his faith. He had lost everything. There was no hope. And this terrible thing he could not tell even to his *kola,* who was down at Pine Ridge waiting to die.

*   *   *

Stormy told his family, "Next ration day I want to try to get a job somewhere around the agency. You can all live better then."

Brings Horses wailed, "We would rather have you with us!"

Elk Rising told her, "Of course we would, but he is a man now, and *he* must decide. He has an education."

Stormy found that he could not leave right away, though. Standing Tree brought over a letter that Sitting Bull had received (not saying how it came—there were no postage stamps on it) and said, "The chief would like to know what this paper says. It is from the rich woman who was thrown off the reservation by the agent, White Hair."

Stormy was delighted. Now he could be helpful! He had some trouble reading her handwriting, but he translated the letter for the chief. It said she was coming to Grand River but would avoid the agency. She told about the place where she would be, just off the reservation, and asked the chief to have two men meet her to act as guides.

The letter was signed C. Weldon.

Stormy wrote an answer for Sitting Bull, confirming this arrangement. The chief had his own messengers.

Mrs. Weldon arrived by a roundabout way, dusty but triumphant, in a wagon with Standing Tree as driver and two other men on horses. Everyone at Grand River watched the wagon come in and had a good look at the white woman. Stormy walked behind the wagon when it passed his family's cabin so that he would be on hand to interpret if the chief needed him. Mrs. Weldon was talking to Standing Tree, who did not understand anything she said. Stormy didn't understand much of what he could hear—she talked too fast and seldom stopped for breath.

Standing Tree pulled up the team in front of one of the chief's two cabins but made no move to help his chattering passenger to the ground, so Stormy helped her, feeling silly. Any woman of his people could get down from a wagon without help, but he knew what a white woman considered normal courtesy.

Sitting Bull came out to greet her with a dignified nod. Stormy interpreted as well as he could when she stopped talking for a moment:

"She respects you, she will read and write letters for you, fight for you on paper with the government. She will make your picture."

Mrs. Weldon was an artist. She had some awkward baggage, including all the things she used for painting pictures.

She talked so much that Stormy could not keep up in interpreting, but the chief said he did not need to know *everything* she said. She had learned a little of the Lakota language and was determined to learn more.

And where would this well-dressed female live? Why, in one of the chief's cabins, of course. Each of his wives had a cabin. Mrs. Weldon did not care which one she lived with.

The chief nodded his thanks to Stormy, dismissing him. Stormy went home, feeling desolate. Sitting Bull had the helper he needed; Mrs. Weldon could read and write English better than any Indian who had studied at Carlisle, and she understood how to deal with the government—perhaps better than the chief did. Those were the important things. For small matters, let her learn Sitting Bull's language.

The entire village was startled at the news that she intended to live in one of the chief's cabins and help cook and keep house. Stormy's mother was downright shocked. She asked quietly, frowning, "Is it this way among white people, that a woman courts a man and moves in with him?"

Stormy sighed. "Mrs. Weldon does not act like any other white woman I ever met! She seems bold, but that is because she is determined to help him. She has lots of money and brought him presents. She makes her own rules."

Sitting Bull gave Mrs. Weldon a Lakota name: Walking Ahead Woman. What he really thought about her he told nobody. He was willing to accept help from anyone who honestly offered it, because once more a commission from Washington was trying to make the chiefs sign a paper to give up a great deal of Indian land. The year before, the Great Sioux Reservation had been greatly diminished and what was left to the Indians was divided into five small reservations. Other chiefs weakened and signed, although Sitting Bull kept trying to strengthen their backbones. Mrs. Weldon and the organization she represented believed he was right.

The whole village talked about Walking Ahead Woman. Of course McLaughlin, the agent, learned from his Metal Breasts, his Indian police, that she was there, but he chose not to notice.

Soon after the white woman came, she received a newspaper—brought by one of Sitting Bull's messengers

—and became furiously angry at something in it. The chief sent for Stormy to interpret. Walking Ahead Woman was too angry to try to speak Lakota. She pointed at something in the newspaper and said, "Look at the frightful lies they tell about me! It is unbelievable that anyone would stoop so low as to attack a poor, defenseless woman this way!"

Stormy could not understand all that, but he read the part she pointed out. At the top, it said: SHE LOVES SITTING BULL. A NEW JERSEY WIDOW FALLS VICTIM TO SITTING BULL'S CHARMS.

The news item was full of mistakes as to facts: Mrs. Weldon's name was spelled wrong, and she was not from New Jersey. It told of her argument with McLaughlin, said she had used "scathing, abusive and threatening language" and that the agent had ordered her to leave the reservation. What angered her the most was this: "She is a great admirer of Sitting Bull, and it is gossip among the people in the vicinity of the Agency that she is actually in love with the cunning old warrior."

The newspaper story went on: "Agent McLaughlin's position in the matter is unquestionably right, especially at this time, as Sitting Bull would surely prove a disturbing element at the lower Agencies during the conference of the Commission on the question of opening the reservation to settlement."

Mrs. Weldon paced the floor as Stormy read to himself. She kept crying, "Vile falsehoods! I am sure McLaughlin did this to humiliate Sitting Bull and to lessen my influence with the Indian Friends in the East! Another newspaper said I came out here to marry the chief. How can they tell such lies?"

Stormy ignored her hysterics. He and Sitting Bull were Lakotas, and they were men. They simply overlooked the ravings of angry women. Stormy translated the newspaper item slowly, as well as he could, not knowing all the English words, and the chief listened impassively.

Then Stormy went home. Later the news was all over the village: the chief, seeing it as his duty to take the distracted woman as his wife, had that night invited her to share his bed, and she had hysterics again, refusing most angrily. But she stayed.

Sitting Bull's two wives told the story with relish. Most of the women thought it was very funny. Most of the men were as puzzled as Sitting Bull at her response to his invitation. After Stormy recovered from the embarrassment of translating the newspaper story, he thought the whole affair was funny.

But his heart was on the ground. He did not feel needed any more at Grand River. Walking Ahead Woman knew the chief's mind about land affairs and could write letters for him. He trusted her judgment in dealing with the government.

Stormy went with his parents and his sister to the agency on the next ration day. They made camp once on the way, the women pitching the canvas lodge with others from Grand River while the men—not as they had done in the old days—cut firewood. Camp had been made in that spot often, and wood was far away. Some families brought theirs in their wagons. Having light wagons instead of pony drags was different, too. It made travel slow, but not so many horses were required as in camp-moving long ago.

During this summer of 1889, probably the first white person among the Lakotas to learn of a portent that great changes were coming was a young woman named Elaine Goodale. She was the newly appointed Superintendent of Indian Education for South Dakota, and she spoke the Lakota language. She had been on an antelope hunt with some Oglalas, because she wanted to understand them better. She noted in her diary for July 23 that her rest had been disturbed by a curious event:

So tired I fall asleep before supper. Later in the night a cry is raised: "A traveler comes!" Chasing Crane, on his way home from Rosebud, is welcomed with supper and a smoke. God, he says, has appeared to the Crows! In the midst of a council he came from nowhere and announced himself as the Savior who came upon earth once and was killed by the white men. He had been grieved by the crying of parents for their dead children, and would let the sky down upon the earth and destroy the disobedient. He was beautiful to look upon, and bore paint as a sign of power. Men and women listen to this curious tale with apparent credence. A vapor bath is arranged, and I fall asleep again to the monotonous rise and fall of the accompanying songs.

Later, she wrote: "No intuition warned me of the bitter grief this self-proclaimed Messiah was soon to bring upon the Sioux."

The Indian Savior had not appeared to the Crow tribe; that was only a rumor. But news of him did reach the Cheyennes and then the Lakotas that summer from tribes farther west. And their world was changed by it.

* * *

A letter for Stormy was waiting at the agency post office. It was from Takes Much at Pine Ridge. He said the family of Morning Rider was small now. The two older sons, Kills Grizzly and Hawk Child, were married. She Throws Him, the baby Grandmother Whirlwind had saved from the she-grizzly, was a fine boy of thirteen winters. Morning Rider's wife, Young Bird, was well. Their daughter, Reaches Far, was married and did not live with them any more.

Takes Much enclosed a short letter to Stormy; Stormy saved that to read later. It was hard to make sense of the English and put it into Lakota, because Takes Much had not been an eager student at Carlisle. Stormy translated the family letter as well as he could, and his parents were pleased, especially his mother. But she shook her head about the omission of Brown Leaf Woman's name, her brother's other wife.

"So she is dead now. Oh, that is too bad. Too bad," Brings Horses said. "You children, don't forget these people. They are your people."

She told them the old stories over again, stories of courage, to make sure they remembered: " . . . and Chief Crazy Horse named my mother Whirlwind 'Saved Her Cub,' because that is what she did," she finished, "but she passed the name on to my baby when he was dying.

"And when this fine young Nez Percé came to us"— she smiled at her adopted son—"we gave him the name Saved Her Cub in honor."

"I am grateful," her adopted son said formally but with a smile. He had a sweet smile.

When Stormy found some privacy, he puzzled over his

kola's letter to him. There was no news in it about Takes Much himself, but the message was very strange:

"I hear story makes afraid. Happy. Say God on earth again. Came before. White men killed him. Now come to save Indians kill bad people. Must learn *wakan* dance. I not know what meaning this."

Stormy shook his head. "I not know what meaning this, either," he muttered. But the message was so important to Takes Much that he had tried to write it also in Lakota, using English letters to make the Lakota sounds as well as he could.

Studying the two versions, Stormy determined what the message meant: News had come to Pine Ridge that made his *kola* happy but was also frightening. The news was that God had come back to earth—according to the churches they had attended at Carlisle, that must mean Christ, the son of God—and said that he had been on earth before but bad men had killed him. Yes, that much was familiar. Now God's son had come back to clear the earth of bad people like those who had killed him but to save all Indians. They must perform some kind of sacred dance that Takes Much did not yet know about.

Stormy was puzzled. He kept the two versions of the letter, thought about them often, and did not tell anyone. He worried about his *kola.* Was he so sick that he saw visions?

12

Where Is the Laughter?

While his father was waiting for rations, Stormy hung around in the trader's store, inconspicuous and staying out of the way. The trader was busy with customers and was gruff with them if they were Indians. So was his helper, a skinny, middle-aged white man who looked as if he drank too much whiskey. The boss and the helper did not get along very well, Stormy noticed, but he thought neither of them got along very well with anyone at any time.

When there was a lull in the trading, Stormy went up to the boss.

"I am looking for a job," he said. "I read and write English and work with numbers."

The boss looked at him coldly. "I've got a man already. Numbers, eh? See if you can add up these bills for goods shipped in."

He scrabbled among papers on a battered table and handed over three pieces of paper with names of merchandise on them, and prices. Stormy had no pencil and would not ask for one. He added the figures in his head while the boss went to straighten some blankets.

"These two are right," Stormy reported. "This is hard to read. If this is a nine, it is all right. If it is a seven, the total is two dollars too much."

The boss stared at it. "Should be a seven. By God, they're tryin' to cheat me! Well, I ain't got any job for you now. Maybe some other time. Not bookkeeping, though. My wife does that."

He turned away, dismissing Stormy, who said, "Thank you," and walked out. He did not think the man would remember his name from the first time he had been there with his father. He had not asked for it this time.

But there was work to be had. His parents had many friends around the agency, among them Big Man and his wife Feather Woman, who had lived there for a long time. They had obeyed the soldiers years before and had come in to the reservation. Big Man cut wood to sell to steamboats and to regular customers at the agency. He had a team of horses for hauling it and was fairly prosperous. Big Man lived in a one-room cabin.

Elk Rising and Brings Horses took Stormy over there to show him off. They found Big Man's wife in her bed place, leaning against her backrest, with one leg bandaged.

Brings Horses rushed into the cabin. "Ah, Feather Woman, you are hurt! What happened to you?" She sat down beside the bed place.

"It is nothing," the woman said. "It was bad, but now it is getting better. I chopped my leg helping Big Man cut wood, that is all. This makes it very hard for him, because he needs me."

Elk Rising was sympathetic. "Yes, it is hard for one

person to handle logs and big branches alone. Is he out now with the team?"

Just then a slim girl slipped in, looking startled, carrying a piece of meat on a sharp stick.

"Our daughter, Bright Water Woman, you know," the woman said. "And this young man with you must be your Stormy, who went away to school. You are welcome here."

Stormy dipped his head to her and stayed out of the way, admiring Bright Water Woman. She was modest, different from his sister, but the same age, he thought. She did not look directly at him. She was not bold. She went quietly about preparing a stew; these people had a small garden with some vegetables growing.

While his parents talked to Feather Woman, Stormy thought about his sister. Her life had been full of disruptions and dangers and anxiety. She lived with hardships worse than this quiet girl had ever endured. She had a right to be different, he told himself loyally. But did she have to be so bold, so saucy? It was not right for a Lakota woman! Bright Water Woman was sweetly old-fashioned.

He listened to her mother telling his mother proudly about the girl and understood that Feather Woman was talking for his benefit, really, because Brings Horses must know these things already:

"Our girl attended the agency school here; she can read and write and speak English."

Bright Water lifted her head and almost spoke, then subsided. Stormy read her mind: *But not very well.*

"You will see my man tonight," Feather Woman promised. "He must be on his way home with wood now."

165

"We will see him," Elk Rising promised. "I always want to see my old friend Big Man."

When it was polite to do so, Stormy left them to go back to the store and watch what his people bought if they had any money, to listen to their puzzled grumbling about how the trader treated them. If one of them complained in broken English and sign, the trader ignored him. If the man kept on trying to protest, the trader flew into a rage and ordered him out.

I don't want to work here, Stormy decided. But in the back of his mind was the idea that maybe he could help his people a little by being there; maybe not.

Before his family went back to Grand River, two days later, Stormy had a job, not in the store but working with Big Man at cutting wood. Feather Woman would not be able to work for a while yet. Even when her wound was healed, he could go on cutting wood. And he could live with Big Man's family in their cabin. He would be paid in money.

For Stormy they hung a privacy blanket because there were no partitions in the cabin. Are they being nice to me, Stormy wondered, or are they protecting Bright Water from me? She should have the privacy blanket around her bed place! But I am the honored guest.

Big Man and his family were trying to do things the white-man way but also clinging to the good ways of the old times as much as they could. Their floor was of packed-down dirt, but clean; Bright Water swept it every day except when there was rain. That summer there was little rain, and the thin crops wilted.

Every day Stormy went out with Big Man to cut and haul wood. He mended the harness, took care of the horses, even built a rough fence around their pasture to save the grass there for winter grazing. There were many horses around, grazing wherever they wished. Stormy picketed Big Man's horses, and as soon as he could he bought a saddle horse of his own, a good spotted pony, black on white. Big Man paid his wages in money.

Stormy stayed out of the cabin whenever possible, and nobody questioned him. Bright Water Woman minded her mother, never looked directly at Stormy, did not joke with him, either, but acted the way Sioux girls of her mother's generation had been taught to act, even to the way of sitting down—in one graceful motion, with both feet on the same side of her—and arose without touching her hands to the ground. There was no furniture. They all sat on the floor.

From various signs, it was made clear to Stormy that he could have Bright Water for his wife if he asked for her. He thought hard about that and liked the idea, but he was in no hurry. He was restless. He had wasted four miserable years. He had lost his faith. Was the rest of his life to be simply a wasting away?

The hard work of cutting and hauling firewood kept him from thinking too much. And he was in a good place to find out what was going on. Every ration day his family came up from Grand River with news; the chief's network of informants found out what was going on at other agencies. More news came from distant tribes, too, because now there were Indians who could write letters.

Stormy exchanged with his own people news that he picked up at Standing Rock, where, in his spare time, he hung around talking with other men. There was hunger and sickness among the people, and not enough to eat.

Crops had failed almost everywhere, even for the poor whites who had moved in to farm on what had been Indian land.

One day in September, Stormy went to the trader's store with his father to see that he was not cheated by the trader, Nagle. The trader was very busy and in a bad temper.

"Hold your horses," he kept telling customers. "I had to fire my helper, so you just wait a minute." Recognizing Stormy, he called, "You, there, come here!"

Stormy sauntered over. "My name is Jack Elk Rising," he reminded the man quietly. He was not "You, there."

Nagle glared at him. "You want to work here?"

Stormy answered, "I have a job cutting wood for Big Man. I like it, and he pays me."

"Damn it, you're wasted at that. Anybody can cut wood. I'll pay you better. Go to work for me now and we'll talk later."

"I will do it because you need help," Stormy told him coolly. "You need some more goods in here." He went to the back room and brought back replenishments for merchandise that he had noticed was gone from the shelves.

To his father he said in Lakota, "I am trying out for this job. I will have supper with you." Elk Rising agreed and walked out.

Stormy kept busy. Late in the afternoon he said to the trader, "You do not have to pay for the work I did today. If you want me to work every day, send a message to my father's lodge while he is here getting rations. We will talk about pay then."

The trader's mouth was open when Stormy walked

out. The only word he said was "Feisty!"

Stormy and his new boss never did get along well, but they managed. The trader laid down certain rules: "You buy everything here, and I take it out of your pay. You steal, and I'll fire you."

"I will keep track of what I buy from you. I am good at numbers. And I do not steal."

"You can sleep in the storeroom. Dunno where you'll eat."

"I will eat and sleep at Big Man's cabin and pay him board. I want every Sunday off, unless it is ration day, and sometimes I want another day too, to go and visit my family at Grand River."

"You sure got your gall," the trader grumbled.

Stormy, with a job and a good spotted pony pastured with Big Man's horses, felt like a man indeed.

Now and then he wrote to his *kola* and received answers with news that was hard to understand. Late in that year of 1889, Takes Much wrote that someone at Pine Ridge had received a letter from a Shoshone, one of those former enemies who lived to the westward. The Shoshone said the son of God was on earth again, and the old, free life was going to return. This savior had promised it. All the Indians would be happy again. There had been a big council at Pine Ridge, and several leading men had traveled to talk to the Shoshones. The heads of the delegation were named Good Thunder and Cloud Horse.

When Standing Tree came up to the agency for rations, Stormy talked to him privately and read him a translation of the letter.

"This is not the first time my friend has mentioned a

savior for the Indians," he told Standing Tree. "The first time was in late summer, when an Oglala brought a rumor from the Crows to Pine Ridge. I thought it was only a story. But now it is a bigger story, coming from the Shoshones, and the wise old men of the Oglalas see enough truth in it so they have sent trusted men to find out more."

"Sitting Bull has heard the story too," Standing Tree answered.

"What is his opinion?"

"He thinks it is only a rumor." Standing Tree thought for a while. "But if it is true, it is a great marvel. It means Wakan Tanka has not forgotten us."

The two men considered in silence. "The missionaries say he sent his son before," Standing Tree murmured. "Maybe they are right. If it happened once, it could happen again. Now."

Stormy was startled but did not show it. "We need him. But I do not think it happened even once."

Standing Tree smiled bitterly. "Neither do I, but I am *willing* to believe."

Before they parted, Stormy asked, "Is Walking Ahead Woman still at Grand River?"

"No, she has gone back East for the winter. She will return next spring."

"Is my mother very sick, that she did not come this time?"

"Don't worry about her. Never very well, but not very sick."

"I will send some more food down from the trader's store. You will take it for me? She likes canned peaches."

"She would like to see you, not canned peaches."

"Now I have my own horse, I can come, taking a day off from my job. Tell her I'm coming soon."

His pony, grass-fed like all Indian horses, with no grain, would be used up for the return trip the next day —but so would he! Stormy felt he was growing soft from work in the store. He lifted and carried heavy boxes and worked long hours but he did not have time to ride very much any more. And he could not go without sleep for two days and two nights and still be able to work. He would not get much sleep at home; they would want to have a feast and to keep talking. Besides, it was after the middle of January; the weather was cold for riding.

He told Nagle he was taking a day off, and rode down to Grand River. He stopped at the cabin of some friends on the way for a little sleep and left a gift of food for his host. His pony had a heavy load of food for his family.

Brings Horses Woman was feeling better but worried about his job.

"Did the trader scold because you took time to visit us?"

Stormy grinned. "Of course. He scolds all the time anyway, like an old woman. Even worse than you, Mother."

He called on the chief, because that was courteous, and talked privately again with Standing Tree. Sitting Bull's network of communications was working very well, as usual. Standing Tree had news.

"The delegation from Pine Ridge to the Shoshones came back, convinced that the Messiah, the Christ, is back on earth. He is of another tribe. His name is Wovoka. The Pine Ridge people want to know more, so they sent a bigger group to find him in a far-off country unknown to us. This time there are the same two leaders, Good Thunder and Cloud Horse, also Short Bull of the Brulés, and Kicking Bear from the Miniconjous—maybe you remember him; he was with us in Canada. And several others went with them. The Shoshones will tell them where to go to meet Wovoka. He teaches a sacred dance, and he makes all things clear."

Riding back to the agency, bowed and blanket-wrapped against the wind, Stormy considered his situation. He could marry Bright Water Woman and set up his own home—even his boss had suggested that, muttering that a young buck was steadier after he settled down. Or he could wait and see what came of the visitation from Pine Ridge to the faraway preacher-prophet, Wovoka.

But what good would waiting do? The more he thought about Bright Water, the more he wanted her—his very own, to stand by him as his mother stood by his father, to understand him and silently comfort him. And he would do the same for her, protect her from the world, dry her tears when she wept. He tried to imagine their children, boys like himself, girls like her.

He had only to ask Big Man for her . . . and to convert to their religion. They were Catholics. He believed in nothing. . . . It would be easy to say he believed. Who would ever know? Not Wakan Tanka, who did not exist. Not the Catholics' God, who did not exist either. . . . But he could lie. The white man had taught him that.

If this Wovoka is the Messiah, he resolved, then maybe I can believe something. I must wait a while and find out more.

The Pine Ridge men who had gone searching for the

Christ would be back in early spring—unless the earth swallowed them up.

When he reached Big Man's cabin—in the morning—tired and cold from the ride, sleepy but with no chance for sleep until that night—he wondered whether his decision was right. Bright Water brought him warm water to wash. She had something ready for his breakfast, knowing that he was already a little late for work. She was silent, attentive, helpful. Her parents had already gone out with the team to bring in a load of wood.

He glanced at her when she was busy. She was graceful, pretty, kind and good. No man deserved any more. He had never touched her, except her hand by accident.

"Thank you," he said, standing up. "Now I will go to work."

He could not be sure she understood his English. In her father's house they all spoke Lakota.

She said in that language, "I will picket your horse. He is tired."

"I am tired, too. I will ride him to the store and picket him there. He can sleep all day. I have to work. Sometimes it is better to be a horse than a man."

Bright Water smiled uncertainly. Stormy could not remember that he had ever heard her laugh. Big Man and his wife and daughter were solemn people. They did not make jokes, and Stormy realized that he missed the joking that went on at home, where members of his family kept misery and despair at a distance with their laughter.

Riding to the store, he considered his situation. Nagle, the trader, paid him very little in money. Nagle hated to part with money. When he had to let go of it, he acted as if the letting go hurt him physically. He paid off in goods wherever possible, thus making a nice profit on every transaction. And he had never stopped trying to cheat Stormy on wages. The total he paid, in a little money and the rest in goods, was higher than Big Man could pay for help in cutting wood, but Stormy had once had a look at his own page in Nagle's bookkeeping system. There were entries there for things he had never bought at all. Stormy kept his own pocket notebook of purchases carefully, and he knew there was a big difference between his total of what he owed and Nagle's total of what he owed.

Stormy would never get out of debt, working for Nagle. So if he married Bright Water he would have to quit that job and go back to work for his father-in-law, working with him, living with the family, seldom getting any change from that household of good people who did not seem to know how to laugh.

Riding to the store, he looked up at the cold sky and asked, "Wakan Tanka, is this how my life is supposed to be?"

He did not receive any answer. He had not expected one.

13

Father, Give Us Back Our Arrows!

Early in that winter of 1889–1890, a good-sized group of serious seekers had set out to find the holy man from whom the tremendous news had come in the first place. They knew his Indian name, Wovoka, but they did not know any of his tribesmen, the Paiutes. They did not even know where he lived. But the Shoshones knew, and the Shoshones lived to the westward, so they rode that way.

These seekers were not adventurous youths but mature men, respected for their judgment. Respected for their accomplishments, too; they had been warriors. They rode with determination toward country where none of them had ever been. Eight or more Lakotas had been joined by some Cheyennes and representatives of other northern tribes.

They rode and camped and picketed their horses; they prayed and slept and cooked and rode again until they found the Shoshones, who had been their bitter enemies not many years before. They were friendly now, united in desperation.

From the Shoshones they received directions and details about this wonder-worker, the Messiah, the Christ
who had come back to earth.

They experienced a wonder themselves. Coming to a
railroad, they sat their restive ponies and watched a train
slow down and stop at a water tank on the prairie. Some
white men were in the last car, cowboys, inquisitive and
good-natured. In sign and bits of broken languages, the
cowboys arranged to have the seekers' ponies carried on
the train—and getting the animals loaded took all their
combined skill, with the scared ponies' hoofs flying. The
cowboys invited the seekers to ride with them in the
caboose. That wonder shortened the journey into the
unknown.

After they left the train, they rode again, west and
south, asking directions when they met other Indians.
They heard strange languages, saw strange customs.

And at a lake in the desert, in the state white men
called Nevada, they found the Paiutes—peaceable Indians whom they would have scorned a few years before.
They found the teacher whose name was Wovoka. The
whites called him Jack Wilson.

Ah, what a day that was! They looked on the dark face
of the prophet, the Messiah!

He preached to them in a great crowd of his followers.
He taught them the sacred Dance of Spirits Returning.
He taught them the sacred songs. He promised that if
they danced as he instructed them, if they sang the songs,
they would greet all the spirits of Indians who were dead,
and the spirits of the endless brown herds of buffalo and
the great pony herds they had lost. Already these were
coming from the West!

He told them he had died and gone to heaven, and his father had sent him back, because the earth was old and worn out, and Wovoka must renew it. The earth would shiver in the spring of 1891 when the grass was an inch high, and new land would push the whites back across the ocean to where they had come from. The believers would be lifted into the air by a sacred feather worn in the hair until it was safe to come down.

The Messiah—many called him the Christ or God, but he did not make such a claim—showed the seekers great wonders. But the Lakotas and the Cheyennes did not all see the same things, or remember the same preachings, when they returned to their reservations in early April of that year, 1890.

They remembered well the songs, they knew the sacred dance, they became the apostles of the new faith among their people, but they overlooked some of the preaching. The Lakota people were, in fact, too desperate to follow all the teachings of Wovoka. And he, an idealistic Paiute who worked on a farm but had been to heaven, did not understand how awful was the suffering of the Lakotas. He had preached, among other things:

"You must not hurt anybody or do harm to anyone. You must not fight. Do right always. Do not tell lies."

These were the same things the white missionaries on the Lakota reservations were preaching, and the whites all claimed to believe in these teachings, but they did not follow them.

The returned seekers began to preach and teach the new religion. Some of them claimed Wovoka was the Christ and said they had seen the nail marks on his hands and feet. Some told of seeing, in Wovoka's holy presence, the spirits of relatives long dead.

They did not want to fight, although they had been a tribe of warriors; they wanted now only to be let alone to dance and pray and make ready for salvation. They did not want to hurt anybody or to tell lies. They wanted to do right—to follow the teachings of the new Christ. But the whites interfered. And that was what made all the trouble.

The Lakotas began to dance. On the Rosebud Reservation the agent sent his Indian police to break up the dancing, and the people fled. The agent had the prophet-preacher, the seeker Short Bull, brought before him. Short Bull promised humbly to stop preaching. *(Do right always. Do not tell lies.)* But he only went to another place farther away and continued.

At Pine Ridge Reservation, the agent stopped the dances near the agency, but the apostle Porcupine, one of the seekers, started them in another camp, on Wounded Knee Creek.

Everywhere there was hunger. In midsummer there was a new cut in the beef ration, and the thin crops withered from drought.

In the dance, the people discarded everything they could that came from white men. The did not wear metal jewelry or carry knives. But they wore clothing and blankets from white men because they had no other, would have no other until the world was made clean and new and all the wild animals returned. Then they would hunt and dress in tanned skins as in the old days, the good days that the older people remembered.

One new thing the Lakotas introduced because of a vision a woman had: a sacred garment, of rare buckskin in a few cases, but usually of cheap, coarse cloth. For men it was a shirt; for women, a dress. Their prophets said it would ward off bullets if the white men began to shoot. (There was talk among the frightened whites that soldiers must be called in. If they came, there could be shooting.) The sleeves and bottom were fringed, and there was a feather attached to the elbows of the sleeves. The garments were painted with sacred symbols, like the sun, a crescent moon, an eagle, and other meaningful pictures. The whites sneeringly spoke of the "ghost dance" and of such garments as "ghost shirts."

The Oglala people at Pine Ridge had been hungry for two years. The family of Morning Rider lived at No Water's camp, about twenty miles from Pine Ridge Agency. The family was small now. There were Morning Rider, son of Whirlwind; his wife Young Bird; his widowed son Hawk Child; and She Throws Him, Morning Rider's son who had been saved by Grandmother Whirlwind. But Reaches Far Girl and Brown Leaf Woman and Hawk Child's wife and Kills Grizzly were dead of white men's diseases reinforced by semistarvation. Even Kills Grizzly, who won his name when he was only a boy! A bear could not kill him, but measles did.

Those who were left were among the first to accept the message of hope that Short Bull and Kicking Bear had brought from the Paiute Wovoka, the Messiah, the Father, the Christ.

Reverently the Pine Ridge people took part in the Dance of Spirits Returning. They had heard the stories told by Short Bull and Kicking Bear: this holy man Wovoka had performed miracles for them. He told them his father in heaven had sent him to earth long ago, but white people had killed him. Now he had returned, because the earth had grown too old and the people were too bad. He had returned *to save the Indians alone.*

He had taught the tribes' emissaries a sacred dance and certain songs. Those who danced would be saved, and the spirits of all the Indians who ever lived would return, with the great buffalo herds and the pony herds and the old, good way of living. This would happen very soon, next spring, and unbelievers would be covered in a landslide of mud.

In preparation for the dance, the men—Morning Rider and Hawk Child and She Throws Him—went through the sweat-lodge ceremony with other men in the morning. After that, priests painted the faces of both men and women who were going to dance, carefully drawing symbols of the sun, the moon, and the morning star. Every person wore an eagle feather tied in the hair, even the women, who had not worn feathers before.

About noon the priests sat down at the base of a small tree with strips of colored cloth tied to the top as an offering. All the other people sat in a circle farther out. A young woman walked to the tree with a bow and four sacred arrows. She shot an arrow into the air toward each of the four directions. A kettle of food was passed around, and each person ate a little from it.

The priests talked for a long time, telling the worshipers what to do and what would happen.

All stood motionless, hands outstretched to the West, from where the promised miracle would come—all the spirits of the dead would come, and the buffalo and the pony herds, all the ghosts returning. They sang the

opening song that the Messiah—the Father—had sent
them through their own emissaries, the song of promise:

> "The Father says so, the Father says so.
> You shall see your grandfather,
> You shall see your grandfather,
> The Father says so.
> You shall see your kindred.
> The Father says so, the Father says so."

Their emissaries had brought this sacred dance from
the Messiah, with the sacred songs, and taught them, and
preached of hope.

Hawk Child's left hand grasped the hand of a sad old
woman; his right hand gripped Young Bird's (she was
trembling); then came Morning Rider, then a woman,
then She Throws Him, then a girl.

The circle moved slowly at first, right to left, then it
moved faster. They sang:

> "Father, I come.
> Mother, I come.
> Brother, I come.
> Father, give us back our arrows."

Faster went the feet in worn-out moccasins, and dust
began to rise. The song changed to jubilation:

> "There is the Father coming!
> The Father says this as he comes,
> 'You shall live!' he says as he comes."

Over and over, until some of them could see the old days coming back, and the men's voices almost drowned out the voices of the women:

"Now they are about to chase the buffalo!
Grandmother, give me back my arrows."

Young Bird was gasping with exertion and emotion. She staggered and fell forward on the ground, her body twitching. The hands that had held hers closed the circle. Things like this would happen, they had been promised. One who was in a trance should not be touched. Young Bird was deep in a vision. But when the circle reached her again, her husband pitied her, because her bonnet and false braid had been loosened in her fall and her scars showed. If she knew that, she would be humiliated. So Morning Rider stepped out of the circle, and it closed behind him. He danced forward and straightened her bonnet and braid. When he returned to his place, it opened for him and the sacred Ghost Dance continued.

One person after another went into the trance and fell, more women than men. For some reason, it was easier for the women, although the men longed just as earnestly to enter into the spirit world. The older ones had all done so at some time in their lives, when they lamented for their medicine, and most of them had done so in the Sun-gazing Dance.

The dance continued, the prayer songs continued, until late at night. One by one, the fallen recovered consciousness to tell what they had seen. Young Bird wandered around inside the circle, crying out, "I saw my sister! I saw her and talked to her, my sister Round Cloud, who died in battle long ago!"

One of the men who fell was old, with thin white braids. Another day when they danced again, they sang a new song that he gave them from his vision of his youth:

> "They have come back racing,
> They say there is to be a buffalo
>   hunt over here.
> Make arrows! Make arrows!
> Says the Father, says the Father."

As they danced, their faith grew and spread. The Father, the Christ, had promised, and those who fell had proof in their trance visions that what he said was true. So hope came again to the desperate, hungry Oglala people at Pine Ridge, and the new faith spread like a grass fire before a roaring prairie wind.

Forgotten by some, unknown to most of them, were many of the preachings of the prophet Wovoka: do not hurt anyone, do not fight, do right always. Do not make any trouble for the whites until you leave them. But they all remembered some teachings: *Do not tell the white people about this. Jesus is now upon earth.* He appears like a cloud. The dead are all alive again, driving the great herds of buffalo and ponies before them. When the time comes there will be no more sickness.

When the earth shakes, the new world is coming. Do not be afraid. I want you to dance every six weeks. Do not tell lies. Do not tell the white people about this! You must not fight.

Walking Ahead Woman was at Sitting Bull's home at Grand River again that summer, this time bringing her young son, Christie. Again she helped the old chief with letters, trying to protect the Lakotas from the government, which kept cutting their rations and cheating them out of the clothing annuity promised by treaty. She worked hard but was very much distressed at the chief's increasing interest in the new religion.

Men who had made the long trip to Nevada to see the man who had originated the Dance of Spirits Returning came to tell Sitting Bull about it. Always a religious man, he studied their words carefully. He would not rush into any big thing like this, but he considered it.

Walking Ahead Woman returned to the East in October, very much worried, hating the dancing. She said it was heathen. Her little boy died on the way, from blood poison—he had stepped on a rusty nail. She was wild with grief. She had lost not only her boy to death but her friends the Lakotas to a shocking, barbaric new faith, and when she railed against it, they had no ears. Catherine Weldon never came back.

PART V

THE
EARTH WILL SHUDDER

1890

14

Suffering Used to End

Stormy's *kola* wrote a careful letter from Pine Ridge. Stormy translated the letter's meaning:

Big dancing here of a religion sent by a Paiute preach he come back to the earth to save the Indians. He was Christ, but the white men killed him long ago. He has the scars, like they told in church. All ghosts of people coming back if Indians dance and sing prayer songs, all buffalo and horses. Some in dance of ghosts returning see the dead. Your relations danced. Young Bird fell down, saw her dead sister was killed in a battle. My friend, almost I believe.

Kicking Bear came over from Cheyenne River, at the invitation of Sitting Bull, and taught the dance and the songs to the Hunkpapas at Grand River. There was great excitement, much joy and hope, for many people went into the trance and had visions:

"I talked with my little boy again—he is not sick or hungry any more. . . . My parents have a fine big lodge with lots of meat. . . . I saw the buffalo coming—ah, the great brown herd coming toward me as in the old days!"

Sitting Bull himself had great power to help people go into the trance. He would go up to a dancing, trembling man or woman and shake a feather, and the person would fall.

Stormy longed to be at home. He was sick of his job, sick of the way the trader cheated people, including himself. When his father came up for rations, Stormy had a talk with him.

"When I went away to school, the chief warned that there would be suffering and no glory, because nobody would see the scars. He was right. But I thought it would end when I came home, and I would live again. I was wrong."

His father moved his head, showing that he was startled. "It does not end? There was always the end to think about when we paid a vow in the Sun-gazing Dance. We knew it would not go on forever."

Understanding each other, they were silent together for a while. Then Stormy spoke:

"My grandmother Whirlwind told me when I was a child about the Land of Many Lodges. On the road to that place, the spirit must pass an old woman who judges whether he can go on. If he has been too bad, she pushes him off into nothing, into forever-nowhere. I do not think I have been bad, but I have been pushed into forever-nowhere.

"At the school, they tried to make us into Wasichus, but there is no place for us. The Wasichus will not let us in."

He wondered whether any Lakota had ever talked that way before, even to a father who understood suffering because of his own scars. But no generation of his people had lived in this nowhere world before.

"How does the trader treat you that is bad?"

"He hired me because I can read and write and do numbers faster than he can. But he does not let me use what I learned, except sometimes to interpret. He knows only a little of our language. I carry the sacks and boxes —anybody can do that, without going to school. I have to buy from him, and I write it down, but he charges me more than the real prices are and gets angry when I show him. Sometime he will take the job away, or I will quit, and then he will not pay the wages he owes me. I know that."

"Your bed place is always waiting in the cabin," Elk Rising assured him and put one arm across Stormy's shoulders in a remarkable display of affection.

Rumors kept spreading. White people were alarmed, fearing the Indians would break out of their restricted reservations and attack. The desperate Lakotas were even more alarmed because they feared the army that might come in. Every agent carefully watched the dance leaders whose message of hope seemed so ridiculous.

There was dancing everywhere and most of the agents were worried. Some reported that their Indians were out of control and would not obey any more. White Hair was not worried, but he was suspicious of everything Sitting Bull did. He thought this new religion was utterly ridiculous. He believed that the Messiah had come to earth almost nineteen hundred years before, had suffered and died for all people, but he sneered at the idea that the Messiah had come back, this time for the Indians alone.

McLaughlin sent some of his trusted Indian police, the

Metal Breasts, to arrest Kicking Bear for being off his own reservation at Cheyenne River. But they could not do it. They returned in a daze, unable to explain their failure. They could not overcome the strong medicine of this priest of the new faith.

As rumors spread that soldiers would be called in to stop the dancing, to cut the people off from their glimpses of the earthly paradise that had been promised, they began to wear the ghost garments every day, not just while they were performing the sacred dance.

In October, the Oglalas at Pine Ridge found they had a new agent named Royer. Stormy, at Standing Rock, received a letter from his *kola:*

"New agent here no good, can't decide what to do. I live with my family now at camp of No Water. We call agent Young Man Afraid of Lakotas. He yell for soldiers. Everybody dancing. I believe. I know."

That was the last letter Stormy ever received from Takes Much.

Stormy attended one day of one dance at Grand River. He took a day off to arrive on Sunday—the day the dance began. He wore a blanket over his work clothes, and as usual he wore moccasins. (Feather Woman had given them to him, but he was sure her daughter, Bright Water, had made them.) His hair had grown to an awkward length, and he looked like any other young Lakota, neither completely Indian nor completely white, but caught in the strange in-between time that had trapped his people.

It was well that he looked that way, because four times on the way down to Grand River he was stopped by suspicious men of his own race who were idling by the road while their saddle ponies grazed. All of them carried rifles.

Three of them knew him and asked no questions. He was just Stormy, son of Elk Rising, on his way to visit his home. Each of these men remarked, "The dance will begin soon."

The fourth was an older man he had never seen before. This man demanded, "Who are you and where are you going?"

"I am Stormy, son of Elk Rising, going to Grand River to see my family. I work in the trader's store at the agency."

The man stared at him. "All right. Are you going to dance?"

"No. I have to go back to the store to work."

"You can go on," the guard told him. "We have to be careful because the Wasichus are dangerous. Soldiers have come to some reservations."

Stormy saw nobody in the camp at Grand River except small children and a few old grandmothers looking after them, with an aged man or two who could not dance, being bent with age. He picketed his pony and walked toward the noise he heard beyond the camp, the woeful chanting of the dancers.

He found his sullen sister, Red Pipe Woman, sitting alone on a hillside, watching them. He was startled to see that she was pregnant and near her time.

She nodded to him as if she had seen him yesterday instead of months before.

"I didn't know you were married," Stormy said.

His sister shrugged. "I am not married. Don't ask me who the father is. Is it any of your business, Brother?"

"No. None of my business. You are still my little sister. I hope it will be a fine, healthy baby."

She said grimly, "So do I."

They sat and listened to the singing in the great, moving circle of reverent, frantic dancers. Stormy recognized the other members of his family: Elk Rising, the limping White Mountain, Standing Tree, Saved Her Cub—all wearing ghost shirts; Brings Horses Woman and the wives of White Mountain and Standing Tree, wearing the shapeless ghost dresses bearing mystic signs. One of the priests officiating was Sitting Bull himself.

The dancers were chanting:

"The whole world is coming,
A nation is coming, a nation is coming.
The eagle has brought the message to the tribe.
The Father says so, the Father says so.
Over the whole world they are coming.
The buffalo are coming, the buffalo are coming.
The crow has brought the message to the tribe.
The Father says so, the Father says so."

Stormy felt himself shiver. Was it true? Was the world coming back to the way it used to be when he was a very little boy?

Stormy saw his mother quiver and shake and fall, then another woman. They lay as if dead on the cold ground. His sister whispered with a sneer, "Our mother says she saw her mother, Whirlwind, in the last dance. Standing Tree's wife saw her child who died. That is why she is carrying moccasins, to give him. White Mountain saw buffalo and killed some."

"If this religion is true," Stormy answered, "these

things will happen in the spring. But you and I will be covered up with mud because we do not dance."

His sister hissed like a snake.

He watched his mother stir on the dusty ground. She staggered, in rising to her feet, as if she could not see well, and cried out something. She ran to his father among the circling dancers and pulled him out of the circle.

Stormy ran down to greet them, concerned about his mother. She was thin and looked older than her age, forty-five. She ran toward her son and daughter, pulling her husband by the hand, acting frantic.

"I saw Whirlwind again in a vision," Brings Horses babbled. "This time she looked sad, but she spoke to me. She said, 'I will meet you in the south.' "

Elk Rising scowled. "What can that mean? She spoke plain when she was with us. She made herself clear when she was alive."

Brings Horses shivered. "I want to go south. I want to go to Pine Ridge and visit my brother, Morning Rider."

"For that we have to ask White Hair for a pass," Elk Rising argued. "It is a rule."

"Nonsense," Brings Horses answered, sounding like her mother.

"Think about it," Elk Rising advised. "When rations are given out at the agency, we have to be there."

But Bring Horses was in a panic; it was hard to calm her. The four of them, parents and the two grown children, walked together to the cabin.

Before Stormy left, he spoke to his father in a low voice: "If you do go south, send me a message. Maybe I will go with you."

When Stormy returned to his job, his boss was in an ugly temper, suspicious and scared, because there was much talk about the ghost dancing, much talk that the Indians were plotting war and destruction. He demanded, "Where were you yesterday? I needed you to unload a freight wagon."

"I told you I was taking an extra day off. I went to see some relatives." Stormy knew that was a lie, about the freight wagon.

"Every chance you get, you go back to the blanket. What good did it do for the gov'ment to spend all that money to send you to school and learn you to act like a white man?"

"Sure, I went back to the blanket. Where else is there for me to go?"

"You don't have to live that way. You could sleep in the back room here."

"Where would I eat?"

"You're just like all of them," the storekeeper snarled. "You want somebody else to figure out everything for you."

From that moment, Stormy hated the man with a bitterness that made him sick.

The storekeeper went on asking questions that were none of his business: "I suppose you got into that crazy dance?"

"No. I have never danced."

"But you seen it. You know what goes on."

Stormy answered, "I never saw it, don't know anything about it," and said to himself, *You and your people taught me how to lie.*

He worked hard all that day, and thought hard at the

same time. He watched the trader give short weight to Indian customers. At quitting time, he went to the trader with his head down, playing that he was ashamed and wanted to make amends.

"You give me good job here," he said. "I will sleep in the back room if you say so."

The trader looked surprised. "Changed your mind, did you? I do say so. I want this place guarded. But if you take anything, I'll know it!"

"I won't take anything," Stormy promised, remembering, *You taught me to lie, you and your people. I won't take anything this time.* "Will you pay me more money if I guard the storeroom?"

"We can talk about that later," the storekeeper growled. Stormy knew how much that promise was worth.

"I made a deal with the boardinghouse," the man said. "You get your meals there, and he takes the price out in trade here at the store. Don't leave you getting much cash wages, of course."

Stormy said, "Well, all right."

The first night he was very vigilant, and the storekeeper, coming quietly, wanting to find him asleep, found him awake and ready to fight. Nothing happened the second night. The third night the storekeeper came again and found Stormy vigilant. After that, Stormy knew it was safe to carry out his plan.

He took two good blankets and put them near the back door under a heap of canvas. He put with them food that would not spoil and hid some ammunition. He longed for a gun of his own, but they were locked up too well. He kept remembering, *You taught us to steal. You stole our lands and our freedom and even our religion. You took away the Sun-gazing Dance.*

By moccasin telegraph, word spread to the faithful—but not yet to the Wasichus—that Short Bull, a Brulé from Rosebud Agency, had preached a sermon at Red Leaf's camp on the Pine Ridge Reservation.

Short Bull, the apostle, one of the seekers who had visited the Messiah down in Nevada, had said the whites were interfering so much that he had decided not to wait until summer for the spirits to return. It would happen very soon!

"We must continue this dance," he said earnestly. "If the soldiers surround you, sing the songs I have taught you. Some of them will fall dead. The horses of the others will sink into the ground. Do not be afraid of the guns. They belong to our father in heaven. He will see that they do no harm." That was because of the protective ghost shirts.

A sacred tree was sprouting, Short Bull said, and the people must gather.

Some day soon, Stormy thought, he was going to have to decide which way to go. The world was pulling him in two directions. It would be easy to let Bright Water's charm and willingness pull him to her father's house to stay. He had never held her in his arms, but his arms ached for her.

His own family, especially his mother, was pulling him toward something unknown in which they had faith and he had none.

But when the time came, he did not have to decide anything. There was only one way to go.

*   *   *

December came. The trader wanted a fire kept burning in the store at night, so Stormy moved his bedding in there but always had it neatly folded and out of sight before the trader came to unlock the front door in the morning.

One day, very early, when Stormy opened the back door of the storeroom, a Lakota he did not recognize was waiting outside, blanket-wrapped, on a bay horse.

The man said softly in their own language, "Soldiers are coming from all over. A message has come to the great chief at Grand River. He must go south, because the Christ is going to appear there.

"If White Hair will not give a pass to leave this reservation, the chief is going anyway. But he is waiting for permission. Some of the people want you to know."

He turned away as Stormy said, "Thanks, friend."

When his boss came in, Stormy said, "The pile of firewood is low. Shall I take the wagon and get more wood from Big Man?"

The trader looked at the woodpile outside, clucked—because, he said, Stormy was wasting it—and ordered, "Go get some more, but hurry up. Remember, I get it cheaper if he don't deliver it, and he has to take his pay in trade."

The young man rounded up the team, harnessed the ponies, and hitched them to the wagon out back, and was able to get the blankets and other things from the storeroom through the back door and into the wagon. He drove to Big Man's cabin, joked a little with Feather Woman (who laughed politely) and left the things there, explaining:

"The trader owes me pay, so I have to pay you with these things. I may not come back here for a few days, but I will leave my things, except my saddle."

Bright Water Woman carried the heavy saddle out to the wagon; she was slender but strong. Stormy said, "Put it on this side," and when she was on the far side of the wagon, out of sight of anyone, he put his arms around her and kissed her mouth. When he drove away, she was staring at him, so he waved good-bye.

He found Big Man three miles away and helped load the wagon.

"The trader owes me pay, but he says I owe him. Now here is the money I have, and I left goods at your house. I may not come back for a few days."

Then he drove back to the store. During the rest of that day, he found opportunities to hide a few more things in his private place in the storeroom—blankets and food and ammunition.

A more serious problem was his horse, still in Big Man's winter pasture. There was no place he could pasture it safely near the agency; the pasture there was for the government's stock. Since he had been eating his meals at the boardinghouse, he had not needed a horse for transportation, and he had not dared to bring it back with the wagonload of firewood. Too many people would wonder what the reason was.

Well, one thing at a time. He could not worry about everything at once. He could not plan very far ahead because he did not know what other people were going to do.

Business at the trader's store was bad; many Indians had moved down to Grand River where the dancing was.

The trader, grumbling, closed the store as soon as it was dark outside.

"Watch out for break-ins," he warned. "Can't trust nobody. Damn fool Injuns, don't they know this savage dancing is crazy? Won't get 'em nothing but trouble."

Stormy was afraid he was right, but he said only, "I don't know anything about it."

Stormy spent part of the evening with two other young Hunkpapas and a half blood at the lodge of one of them, who was married. They played poker for matches, because none of them had any money, and talked mostly about rumors they had heard about the spread of the Dance of Spirits Returning. It was going on at every reservation now. People who fell in trances had wonderful reunions with dead friends and relatives. The only time the men laughed was when they talked about how scared the white people were.

"Soldiers are coming everywhere," one man warned, and they did not laugh any more.

Stormy went back to the store, spread his blankets, stoked the stove so the fire would keep, and went to bed early.

He awoke in darkness at the sound of a coyote howling faintly at the back door, where no coyote should be. Grabbing the revolver that the trader had lent him to scare robbers with, he walked softly to that door and made a sound like a crow. The coyote laughed softly—his brother, Saved Her Cub. Stormy unlocked the door, let him in, and lighted the lantern.

"They have left Grand River, heading south," Saved Her Cub said. "I know a short way to catch up with them in two days."

"I have some food to take along, and new blankets. My

saddle is here. But my horse is in Big Man's pasture." Stormy began to wrap the things he was taking into two packs.

"Your horse is in some brush near here with mine," his brother assured him, with a sidewise glance of his laughing eyes. "All my life I have listened to stories the old men told about stealing horses from the enemy. I had no problem. And there is no snow to make tracking easy. But I could not go into the house to bring your white-man suit."

Stormy laughed shortly. "I won't need that."

Never again would he need it. There would be no returning. Stormy recalled a phrase in English: *We are burning our bridges behind us.*

He left everything as it was in the store, hoisted his saddle over his shoulder, locked the door, and took the lantern with him after blowing out the flame. For December, the night was not very cold.

Stormy's pony had a notion to buck—he had not been ridden for a while—but Stormy twisted his nose.

The two young men rode off together, leaving Standing Rock for the last time. Stormy could feel his brother's happiness and excitement, as if this were all a game.

"You have a rifle on your saddle," Stormy remarked. "I have only a revolver. There is ammunition in these packs though."

"Our father has a rifle for you, a good one. New. From Sitting Bull." There was laughter in his voice. "His white woman gave him lots of money before she became angry and went away, went home. Did you think he spent it all for tobacco and candy?"

Stormy laughed aloud. Suddenly he was an Indian, and free, riding to danger, riding to disaster, and life was as it should be. Like the generations of his grandfathers, he was doing something dangerous, something expected of him, doing it of his own free will. He felt no guilt at all about taking what he wanted from the trader's store. Like his grandfathers and their grandfathers, he had simply taken something from an enemy.

Saved Her Cub followed his thoughts and glanced toward him. Even in the darkness, Stormy could tell that his eyes were laughing as he said, "Those rifles at the trader's will be covered up by mud pretty soon. If we run into soldiers, their bullets will not hurt me. But you have no ghost shirt. I am wearing mine."

"Do you really believe that?" Stormy burst out. "You have danced, but do you believe God has come again and that all the dead are returning, and the herds of buffalo?"

"Almost I believe," his brother replied. "For our mother's sake I say I do."

Stormy said in English, "My God!" and in Lakota, "You are a brave man."

"No more than you. You do not even almost believe. But you are here, and you can never go back. Are you sorry to leave your girl behind, not telling her?"

"No. . . . Yes, but she would not understand. I am glad I did not marry her." Suddenly remembering Red Pipe Woman, he asked, "Did our sister have her baby?"

"She was having pains when I left."

"But she will travel anyway, so soon?"

His brother shrugged. "Our women have done it before. She is a Lakota. Brings Horses will make a pony drag."

It was broad daylight and they were safely away from people when they stopped to rest the horses and eat something from their packs. They did not build a fire.

"Should we sleep now?" Stormy suggested. "And ride at night?"

"We'll sleep when the sun gets *so* high." His brother pointed. "My horse will need it then."

"Did you ride him all the way from Grand River? You'll kill him."

Saved Her Cub gave him the sidewise glance. "No, I had this one with friends halfway between. I knew this day would come. If you didn't, you must be part white man."

"Don't insult me. I have only been associating with the wrong people. How do you know this trail so well? Have you been over it before?"

"No, never. But I have talked to other men. I associate with the right people. And I know where this trail meets the one that our family is taking toward the south."

The brothers laughed together. Ah, it was good to be free and in danger!

When the sun was *so* high, they came to a small stream. They watered their horses and staked them off the dim trail to graze and sleep. The young men built a small fire, warmed some food, and ate, then rolled in their blankets and slept a few hours.

When they started on, Saved Her Cub spoke gravely:

"I want to warn you. Our mother keeps talking about her mother, Grandmother Whirlwind. She wants to be sure I remember her, because we are going to meet her in the south."

Stormy was startled. "Brings Horses must be sicker than I thought. You could not remember Whirlwind! She died before you joined our family in Canada."

"Oh, I remember her well. She has become my grandmother, too."

Stormy thought about that for a while, worrying about his mother.

"Make no mistake," Saved Her Cub said, "Brings Horses *knows* she is going to meet Whirlwind in the south, because of the vision she had during the dance. And they *will* meet, whatever becomes of the rest of us."

"All right. I believe you. . . . Do you remember the battle your people had with the soldiers before you became my brother? They thought you were about four years old."

Saved Her Cub remembered in a dreamy voice as the horses moved along the trail. "I was afraid and hurt. I could not understand what any of you said, because we spoke different languages. But your people were kind, and I was not afraid any more. Your mother became my mother, because my first mother had been killed in the battle. So I am not a Nez Percé any more. I am a man of the Lakotas."

"And both of us," Stormy assured him, "remember Grandmother Whirlwind very well, because our mother wants us to remember."

They rode along in companionable silence for a while. His brother said thoughtfully, "When you went away to the Indian school, that was a brave thing. I have always been proud." Again the sidewise glance, but without laughter.

"That was not brave. I was afraid. But I thought it was my duty. It was wasted."

"You were afraid, but you did it. That is bravery. Stop arguing. You cannot make me be *not* proud."

Stormy's heart felt lighter. He smiled. This was a brother indeed!

15

The Ghost Shirts Will Protect Us

They rode in high spirits. There was no cabin or lodge in sight, had been none for hours, when Saved Her Cub said, "Look, a horse!" Stormy spotted it at the same instant—a bay with four white feet and a blazed face, a rather small gelding, with marks of use on it but no broken tether rope.

"That pony looks lonesome," Saved Her Cub remarked, riding cautiously toward it.

"It's small, not an American horse," Stormy objected. "Do we want to take it from one of our own people?"

"But we will take it along," his brother coaxed. "Maybe we will meet the owner." He began to make soothing sounds to the grazing animal; it looked like a good four-year-old.

Stormy smiled. "Of course we will, because horses should not be alone. See how unhappy he is. There are tears on his face." He rode to the other side, glad he had a rope handy, and they caught the lonesome horse with no trouble and rode on, leading him, laughing softly.

"We will catch up with our family soon," Saved Her Cub promised. "We will cut their trail soon."

They had not yet cut the trail when Stormy pulled up short. "I saw something move in the brush to the left."

Saved Her Cub pulled out his rifle, then sighed with relief. "A range cow and her calf from last spring—nice big calf. We need meat. You keep the cow off if she interferes; use my rope. I'll get the calf. The cow probably doesn't want it around anyway."

He put his rifle away and rode circuitously toward the big bull calf. Stormy made a loop in the other rope and prepared to throw it over the cow's horns and pull her off her feet if he could. She liked her calf but did not fight for it very hard. Stormy let her chase him and his horse, luring her away.

Saved Her Cub leaped from his saddle, grabbed the calf's head and threw it on its side. Then he stabbed the calf in the throat and kept it down as it struggled convulsively, trying to rise, trying to live.

Stormy rode back and said, "It had better bleed well. We do not want to leave a bloody trail behind us."

The cow came trotting, and Saved Her Cub leaped on his horse out of her way. She nuzzled her dying child and bellowed in mourning, but she did not fight when they loaded and tied the carcass on the lonesome horse. The horse fought, though, hating the smell of blood. The young men subdued him without exchanging any words. They were spotted and even soaked in the calf's blood.

They worked as a team, each knowing the other's mind. They were bringing meat and more than meat

—here was a present for their mother, a chance for her to show gleefully her old skill at butchering.

"Maybe," Stormy remarked, "our sister will learn something useful from watching her. I wonder if the baby is a boy or a girl."

Now they cut the trail of their family—three horses, ridden; one packhorse; another horse with travois poles dragging, no doubt Red Pipe Woman on the travois with her child.

Stormy inquired, "Why are there *three* horses with riders?"

"Oh, White Mountain is with them. Didn't you know?"

Stormy answered crossly, "I am not a good tracker at long distance, and I cannot read minds all the time."

His brother laughed at him, and Stormy forgot his anger.

He kept thinking how dangerous was the situation of the family. His father must be riding first, watching for trouble, such as soldiers coming toward them, with White Mountain last, looking over his shoulder for trouble following from Grand River.

There were others fleeing toward the south, ahead on the other trails, and perhaps behind them. And everywhere there were soldiers, called in to stop the Dance of Spirits Returning.

With so few animals, the family could not have taken along very much in the way of a lodge, bedding, cooking pots, and food. But they did not have very much to take. They must be suffering in the cold nights.

"Ah, they will be pleased with us!" Stormy said.

His brother began to sing softly a song from the sacred dance:

"They have come back racing,
They say there is to be a buffalo hunt over there.
Make arrows! Make arrows!
Says the Father, says the Father."

Stormy asked, "Do you really believe that?" and his brother replied, smiling, "What else is there to believe?"

Stormy nodded. There was nothing else.

Stormy was ahead when another confused trail cut into the one they were traveling. He held up his hand.

"Something wrong," he warned. "Here are wagon tracks—a wheel is wobbly—and a few horses. I can't tell. Coming in from the east."

His brother rode to look. There was little snow, the ground was hard, the tracks were difficult to sort out.

"Some people from Grand River," he decided, "who left by another way. Some left before us, but they go slow because of the wagon."

"Too many of them and not enough horses?" Stormy suggested.

"Paints Black and his family," his brother guessed. "They are very poor. His old father can't ride; he is too old and full of pain. The old man would be in the wagon, with maybe two children."

They caught up with Paints Black before sundown. He was desperate, but he met them with an aimed rifle, protecting his family. His woman was driving the bony team that pulled the rickety wagon. When she turned to face them, she aimed a rifle, too.

The young men stopped a prudent distance away, making the sign for peace.

"I am Stormy, son of Elk Rising," the older brother shouted. "This is my brother."

Paints Black and his woman laid down their guns.

The man explained, "My father did not want to come, but we would not leave him. The wagon is bad, we have to keep going off the trail, looking for easier ways. Your family can't be very far ahead."

For courtesy, Stormy rode to the wagon to speak to the old father, but he was apparently asleep, with his blanket over his head. The two small children huddled together far from him, not saying anything.

"You ride ahead and tell your family we are coming to camp tonight," Paints Black suggested, looking hard at the calf slung on the lonesome horse.

Of the two young men, Stormy was ahead and Saved Her Cub behind him, leading the lonesome horse with its load of meat, when they caught up with the family. The first glimpse Stormy had made him shudder: up ahead, White Mountain sat his saddle, aiming a rifle straight at him.

He called, "White Mountain! We have brought meat!"

His brother rode up beside him to show the packhorse. White Mountain shouted to the family and rode back to meet the young men, waving the rifle in greeting.

"Ah, good! We need more food." They kicked their riding horses into a fast trot, with the led packhorse following because he had no choice.

The others had gathered in a tight little group; Elk Rising had his rifle ready to protect his women, but he shouted with joy when he recognized his sons.

Stormy glanced at his sister, lying on a travois. She was flat now, but there was no baby in her arms.

He greeted her: "My sister."

"My son was born the day before we started," she said, "but he never breathed." Tears welled into her eyes. "He was to be something of my very own. Now I have nothing."

"You are alive," Stormy reminded her. "You are with us who love you." Then he turned to greet his mother.

She said firmly, "Everything is going to be all right. We are together, and we are going south to meet the Christ. A sacred tree has sprouted there, and we will find the place. I will butcher your kill as soon as we camp. A fine animal!"

Stormy greeted his father. None of them even dismounted. Elk Rising warned, "We must go a little farther before we camp. Paints Black will find us."

As they went on, White Mountain rode ahead as scout, with Saved Her Cub last, watching behind them. Stormy, leading the packhorse that carried the slaughtered calf, rode beside his mother, whose horse pulled the pole travois on which Red Pipe Woman lay; there was some baggage with her. Their packhorse, a weary old mare, sometimes lagged behind until someone reminded her with a quirt or a knotted rope to hurry.

Stormy noticed that the gaunt face of his mother, Brings Horses, was transfigured. She glowed with faith and joy. By long custom, Brings Horses had been eating very little because food was scarce, leaving all she could for the men, who were the protectors, and for her pregnant daughter, keeper of the next generation of the people.

They did not talk very much but listened for horses. This was the way small parties used to travel long ago in enemy country when they were a free people and all the world was theirs.

Stormy was uplifted by an emotion that was strange to him but not quite beyond his experience. He remembered far back to his childhood, to a time when he had not learned how bad things could be. Then he knew what the emotion was. It was joy.

They camped off the trail in a brushy coulee. Brings Horses took charge of skinning and butchering the calf, showing off her skill with vast delight, ordering the men to help her—she was the matriarch now, doing the work to which she had been born, the work of which she had long been deprived.

The men smiled inside, behind the grave masks of their faces, enjoying her pleasure, meekly accepting her grumbling. She was very hard to please. Even Red Pipe Woman sat and watched intently, saying "Yes, Mother" and "I understand, Mother" as Brings Horses demonstrated and scolded and taught.

"You will learn to do this as well as I do," Brings Horses promised. "Because the buffalo are coming, and we will have much butchering to do. But not on stiffened animals like this one—it is easier when the animal is newly killed, but harder with a full-grown buffalo, it is so big, and it has a huge hump here on the back so it can't be turned over by one or two women. Ah, they are big and beautiful, the great buffalo! How we will feast! And you, my daughter, will learn to tan hides and to make a fine lodge of them. My mother will help us, Whirlwind will help us. She taught me well, but it is so many years now, I have almost forgotten some skills she taught me."

Elk Rising said gently, "I think we should eat well tonight, but we should not feast yet. We do not know how far this meat will have to take us."

The darkness was almost total when they heard the family of Paints Black wailing. That was the sound—the wailing of grief—Paints Black singing his sadness in a deep voice, and his wife screaming. Stormy seized his grazing horse and his rifle and rode back along the trail. The others took up positions of defense, after covering the fire.

As Stormy approached the newcomers he could hear even the children shrieking. He shouted reassurance.

Paints Black and his wife both talked at once, so it was hard to understand their story:

"The old father was not asleep in the wagon. He was dead! He had his knife, and he cut his veins—his wrists and his throat—to set us free so we can go faster. Ah, Antelope was a brave man, a good man! He gave up life for us!"

Stormy spoke the most comforting words he could think of: "So also did my Grandmother Whirlwind, long ago, because she did not want to use strength that the people needed. She is honored for it. And your old father will be honored for this great gift. Everybody will learn of it and honor him."

He could not have said anything more comforting. It was well remembered that Grandmother Whirlwind had starved herself.

"Now come and eat," he invited. "This is something you must do."

The meal was not festive, after all, but everyone ate well, because they had been hungry for a long time.

Then, quietly, the women—even Red Pipe Woman helped—wrapped the old man's frail body tightly in his blood-stiffened blanket still in the wagon. Paints Black and Elk Rising found a gully with some big rocks in it. There were no trees big enough to hold the body off the earth.

White Mountain hitched a horse to the wagon and drove to the gully, the others following in loud and proper mourning. When the horse was unhitched, the men lifted the body down and overturned the light wagon to cover it. They rolled rocks around the wagon to weigh it down. And so they left Antelope, that brave man, and returned to camp, sorrowing.

There was now a serious problem of transportation, but they slept through the rest of the night hours before attempting to solve it.

In the morning Red Pipe Woman announced, "Today I will not need a travois. That can take the two children and some baggage. I will ride a horse."

"You had a hard time in the birth," her mother said. "Just one more day on the pony drag?"

"I am a Lakota woman," Red Pipe Woman insisted with sturdy pride.

They had to decide which horse was for her. The two young men tried out the lonesome horse, one twisting his nose to keep him quiet while the other fought the bridle onto him and cinched on a saddle. Stormy leaped on, the horse bucked, and on the third buck Stormy went flying.

"Our sister will not ride that one!" he announced, rubbing his hip.

"Now little brother will show you how to ride a horse,"

Saved Her Cub promised—and he did. He tired out Lonesome Horse. The animal had been ridden before, but was skittish.

"Sister will ride my horse, because he is tired and won't fight," Saved Her cub suggested. "I need my saddle. She will ride on a blanket."

There were barely enough horses, but nobody had to walk, although the women had much to carry and their horses were not good.

As they rode along, Brings Horses worried aloud, voicing her major preoccupation: "Stormy and my daughter have never joined the sacred dance. They must do that as soon as possible, so they will not be swallowed up in mud with nonbelievers, or as some say, turned into little fishes."

They rode with all senses alert; Stormy realized that he had never before felt so much a part of the living world around him or so close to danger or so glad to be a man, one of the Real People. He admired his family and each member of it. He and his brother had been soaked in the dying calf's blood, now dried. He was a bloody savage, as had been said of him when he wore white man's clothing and had his hair cut short. He wanted to yell with jubilation, but yelling was dangerous. The party was making enough noise, although nobody spoke.

Up ahead, Elk Rising held up his arm in a signal to stop. He had heard something—a horse coming, fast. The men checked their rifles.

The startled rider, a middle-aged Indian, pulled up his horse and spoke in Lakota: "Let us talk, friends." He wore a ghost shirt.

Hastily he told them his name. "I am going to see Sitting Bull at Grand River. Back there"—he motioned with his head—"everything is bad. Soldiers everywhere. Our people are divided. Some who dance have burned the cabins of those who do not dance, and taken their cattle. Short Bull and Kicking Bear and a lot of Brulés went to a place in the Bad Lands called the Stronghold, where nobody can get them. They have plenty of meat. They are dancing.

"Hump and Big Foot had a great dance going on Cheyenne River. But Hump turned traitor and is now a scout for the white soldiers. Big Foot is still leading his people, they are still dancing, waiting for the earth to shake."

Elk Rising asked, "What is the shortest way to Big Foot's camp?"

The other man drew directions in the dirt with a twig, showing streams and obstacles. "The people are mixed —from various agencies. Wear your ghost shirts for protection against bullets, but under something else before you reach Big Foot, because of soldiers."

Elk Rising assured him, "Chief Sitting Bull will welcome any news. We are from Grand River. Many people left before us. My son, that man there, came from Standing Rock Agency. That place lost many people because of the disturbances. We are grateful for the information."

The rider mounted his horse and galloped on.

Brings Horses became almost frantic after he left. "Which is closer, the Stronghold in the Bad Lands or Big Foot's camp on the Cheyenne River? I don't know these things, but we must dance, because Stormy and our daughter must be saved when the earth shudders!"

The younger members of the family glanced at one another sadly, but Elk Rising was patient. "No, my woman, you do not understand. We can't get to the Stronghold, so it doesn't matter where that is. We must protect ourselves until we reach Big Foot's camp. They will take us in."

White Mountain murmured, "Soldiers all over, and we are few. But we know what the smallpox sickness looks like." He smiled and touched the pitted scars on his own face.

Elk Rising nodded and brought out his paints. With a steady hand he painted the red horror of smallpox on the face of his daughter and a little of it on the face of his older son, in case Stormy might be recognized by Lakota scouts with the soldiers. They would not care to come close to a family that carried such sickness. Paints Black spotted his woman's face, smiling grimly.

They did meet one small bunch of Blue Coats and a Lakota scout with their horses trotting. The soldiers' officer shouted, but the family pretended not to understand anything. The scout came forward officiously to interpret, but when he took a look at Red Pipe Woman's face as she threw back her shawl, he yelled a warning and pulled his horse back. The soldiers rode far out to pass them. Stormy heard one of them laugh and say, "Maybe they'll give it to all the rest."

As the family rode, Brings Horses counted on her fingers how long it had been since they had seen their Oglala relatives. Nine winters. Nine winters since the Oglalas, including her brother Morning Rider, had been put at Pine Ridge and the Hunkpapas who came down from Canada with Sitting Bull had been taken to Fort Randall.

The only word she had had of Morning Rider's family was in the few letters her son Stormy had received from his *kola* down at Pine Ridge.

She spoke to nobody in particular: "We will find them. We will hear the voices in the dancing. Listen. I think I hear them."

But nobody else could. She guided her horse so as to ride beside her daughter and called, "Stormy, come here." To both she said, "I want you with the rest of us when the spirits come. All you have to do is dance, and then you will believe and be saved."

Stormy looked at her with pity; she did not see why. He answered, "Yes, I will dance." Even Red Pipe Woman agreed: "I will dance."

"Then you will have your baby son who did not live long enough to breathe, and everything will be as it was in the old days."

For once, Red Pipe did not say she was tired of hearing about the old days.

Brings Horses rode on, content and serene in her faith.

My mother did great things. I do small things, she remembered, and spoke to Red Pipe: "Beginning tomorrow you shall wear my ghost dress to protect you from the white men's bullets if there is trouble. I don't need it. If my ghost is one of those that returns, we will not be separated very long."

She was confident and even merry. Elk Rising looked at her in a worried way, but there was no reason. She had faith enough for all of them.

16

Lakotas' Hearts Are Big

That night as they huddled around their small fire, Brings Horses said suddenly, "I don't understand why the soldiers have come."

"Because they are afraid of us," Elk Rising answered. "White men are afraid of all Lakotas. They think we will join together and attack them now that we are united in the sacred dance."

"The white men have their religion," Brings Horses said. "Some Lakotas believe in it from the missionaries. Stormy, what do they believe? They taught it to you at school."

"They say the Great Mystery sent his son to earth a long time ago to save everyone, but some bad people killed him, so he went back up to his father in the sky. The whites pray to the Great Mystery and his good son, and sometime the son will come back to judge the living and the dead."

"Of course," Brings Horses agreed. "That is all perfectly reasonable, so why is there any argument about religion? That is what the Dance of Spirits Returning is about. The good son is on earth again. He is a Paiute named Wovoka. He told that story to Kicking Bear and Short Bull and the others who went to see him. He has come back, but this time only to the Indians, because the white men treated him so bad. And soon he will be here and all the ghosts will live again. We pray and take part in the dance so we will be saved when the whites sink into the mud."

Stormy replied, "I never understood why they think their religion is the only true one and everything we know must be wrong. Their minds are small and their hearts are stone. Religion is good even if it is different. But the whites don't live the way the good son of the Great Mystery told them to live. They talk about it in church but they don't do it. That much I learned."

Brings Horses said, "Listen, do you hear the singing?" But it was only a cold wind in the brush of a coulee.

It was long before Brings Horses could sleep that night. She kept thinking about religion. The whites could accept only one, and all others were wrong. The Lakotas' hearts were bigger. They were forbidden to worship the Great Mystery with the ancient Sun-gazing Dance, but the older people still believed in everything it stood for. When they learned about the new Christ who was a Paiute Indian, they did not throw away the old faith. They accepted the new faith, too. They accepted even the idea that in the ghost dance women were the equals of men. In fact, more women went into the trance and had visions. Perhaps that was because the women ate very little when food was scarce.

Just before she slept, she made a resolution. She would teach the songs to Stormy and Red Pipe as they rode. Then her son and daughter would be ready to join in the dance as soon as they found one, and they would all be saved together. There was very little time, she was sure.

It was hard to chant properly to suit the movements of a horse that trotted, but they were doing it the next day when something happened. White Mountain, Elk Rising's brother, was guarding the rear of the little procession, and was not singing, when he heard the pounding hoofs of many horses coming fast behind him. He shouted a warning and turned to face danger, holding his rifle ready. Almost he yelled, as in the long-ago days, *"Hoka hey!* It is a good day to die!" But it was not a good day for women to die.

The front rider reared up his horse in astonishment and cried, "White Mountain, almost brother!" He was Standing Tree, with maybe twenty-five men behind him, stern-faced and angry. No women. So it was a war party. In these days of captivity, a war party? They were traveling light, with almost nothing for food or comfort, but they were well armed.

White Mountain shouted, "Standing Tree! Is there trouble?"

Stormy rode back and was silent at his uncle's elbow.

All the warriors were anxious to talk, all were horror-struck. "The Metal Breasts came from Standing Rock to arrest Sitting Bull. There was a fight in his cabin. He is dead—the chief is dead, with his closest friends and his son and some of the traitor Metal Breasts. The soldiers are there. We are going to the Bad Lands."

Elk Rising roared in horror. "Our chief is dead? Murdered by his own people, traitors?"

He began such a wail of grief and shock as his family had never heard him utter before. They joined him. They were broken. Their hearts were on the ground, bloody and trampled.

Standing Tree motioned for silence. "We have told you. We must ride faster than you can. We were in the fight with the soldiers. Some may be behind us. Some of our people are certainly behind us, coming as fast as they can—with women and children. We are going to the Stronghold in the Bad Lands. The rest will try to find refuge somewhere."

The fleeing warriors from Grand River galloped on, yelling.

Brings Horses did not wait for a decision from the men. She cried out, "South! We must hurry south before the earth shakes!"

They hurried on, stopping late to camp, and then only because their horses were so tired. The men took turns standing guard that night, with the guard snatching up handfuls of long, dry grass to take along for the horses. There had, until now, been a kind of frantic gaiety in the small party of travelers. Now there was only despair.

At noon the next day, a Hunkpapa boy of about fifteen caught up with them on a spent horse. He was shouting, "Wait! Help us!"

He was almost too exhausted to stand. One of the women brought him a drink of water, another ran to a stream with a bucket to get water for the horse.

"Help us," the boy gasped, sitting down in the thin snow, drinking the water. "Women and children from Sitting Bull's camp. Few men. Enough horses, but worn out. We left without anything except what we could grab."

They all knew him, of course. His name was Joe, and his father was a close friend of the chief.

"My father was killed in the fight," he gasped. "One of the Metal Breasts shot him. My mother is coming."

Elk Rising said, "We will wait. White Mountain, Saved Her Cub, go back and help his people."

The women were already unpacking the food. Joe fell sideways, exhausted, asleep before he could eat.

There were almost forty in the refugee party after the wailing followers caught up. They could not go on right away; the horses had to sleep and graze or they would die. The women slept, too, shivering, because they had fled in disorder without blankets for bedding. Children slept, whimpering.

In all this confusion of exhaustion, hunger, and help-lessness, one gaunt and weary person stood out: an old man, worn beyond his strength but undefeated, like a tree at timberline, gnarled by struggle to survive, but surviving. They all knew him well, a fighting man long past his prime, a quiet man—Horse Breaker.

He did not take charge of the whole group now that they were together. He went to sleep, tired out.

Elk Rising assigned the young men to take turns on the night watch, one tending the horses, the other guarding the people. He spoke to the young men quietly:

"There is our leader because he is wise, and I am sure he has been this way before. I will speak to him in the morning. His words are few but full of wisdom."

The young men, taking turns during the night at piling

up dry grass for the horses, watching and listening with rifle at the ready, longing for their chance to sleep a little, were proud to be awake and uncomfortable and necessary to their people. Stormy exulted in silence: "I am a man of the Lakotas! This is part of what it means!"

In early morning the young men could sleep while older men made plans. Yes, Horse Breaker was willing. He would lead them.

"I have been this way before. White Hair the agent did not know. I know where Hump's Miniconjous have their permanent camp, and Big Foot's Miniconjou band, too. They have all been dancing. Many of the Oglalas from Pine Ridge joined them to dance, because they did not dare on their own reservation. Now there will be trouble everywhere, because word of the killing of Sitting Bull will soon reach everywhere."

Horse Breaker was a good chief for the refugees. The other old men made suggestions but did not argue. The young men listened with respect.

"It is not far now, if we are lucky and the Miniconjous have not moved," he told them. "But we will all suffer, because it is cold and we cannot build shelters where there is no timber, and we have little food or clothing. Some of the young men must walk sometimes, because they are stronger than the women and our horses are few and worn out. Many moccasins are worn out."

Stormy stepped forward to be recognized; then he spoke: "I brought good shoes that I learned how to make. I can walk. Maybe my brother can wear them sometimes."

Horse Breaker looked approving. "One man on a horse, at a slow trot, another holding the stirrup to help pull him along—yes. But we must not spread out far along the trail."

When everyone was ready, he let those two young men go first. The shoes did fit.

Cold and with half-empty bellies, the women frightened, a few children whimpering, they headed south. They crossed creeks and rivers, resting sometimes from exhaustion, letting the bony horses graze and doze.

Brings Horses Woman was always cheerful, remembering that her mother, Whirlwind, had been strong in harder times than this.

"There will be no blizzard," she remarked. "Sitting Bull promised that, and you know how he could foretell the weather. Some said he even controlled it. He promised an open winter so we could dance all the time, awaiting the coming of the Great Holy's good son and all the spirits returning."

She said this often to weary women, and they were strengthened. They struggled onward, suffering, enduring, because they remembered with pride that they were Lakotas, a great people.

Stormy was the first to spot a bunch of Indians ahead. He was riding, with Saved Her Cub running at the stirrup.

"Hold!" Stormy shouted. "There are people on the other side of the river." They waited for the other refugees to catch up.

Old Horse Breaker came up and squinted across. "This is Cheyenne River, and right over there Cherry Creek flows into it," he said. "Now who are those Lakotas?"

Elk Rising joined him, and Paints Black, the oldest

men, the wise leaders. Across the river, men made the sign for peace and the sign for Miniconjou. They signed, "Come over and talk." Some of them pranced their horses; they were excited, not afraid of trouble.

"Time to talk, not to fight them," Elk Rising suggested.

Horse Breaker agreed. "We will go and leave the helpless ones here to build fires and try to be warm. We are all well armed? Yes. And some of the women have rifles. All have knives. The women need protection, so the young men will stay—Stormy, Saved Her Cub, and those who came with me."

The older men rode across the river, their horses' hoofs breaking through the thin ice. The younger ones, a little jealous but aware of their heavy responsibility as protectors, watched in all directions while the women scavenged for firewood.

The women were afraid and did not hesitate to show it, chattering among themselves: "But who are those people? Friends, as they say, or enemies who lie?"

On their own side of the river, the young men saw riders coming at a businesslike trot—Indians, armed, signing for peace. But it was a tense time. Who were these new men? Young men, all of them, ten young men, rifles ready.

"Cover my back," Stormy said and rode to meet them.

The front rider signaled "Stop" to those behind him and waited for Stormy to speak.

"We are from Grand River. We are Hunkpapas," Stormy told him briefly.

"We are Miniconjous," the front rider replied. "Chief Big Foot sent us to look for you when he learned that

Sitting Bull was dead and some people were coming this way."

"We are looking for Big Foot's camp, or Hump's, where we heard the sacred dance continues. Who are those across the river?"

"Chief Hump is there, for one. He surrendered to the white soldiers. He is trying to persuade others to surrender, too."

"It looks as if they might fight over there." They could hear the shouting and see the riders swirling, working up anger.

"It may come to that." The young Miniconjou looked as if he wouldn't object at all to a good fight—as long as he was in it. "Big Foot is camped only a day's ride from here. The people were dancing when we left. We will go across the river and see about things there."

Stormy thought that was a good idea, because some of the noise over there was singing—he recognized angry warriors singing their death songs, they were that close to starting a fight.

His brother said, "I would like to go over there."

"You will stay here, and so will I, because those are our orders," Stormy told him shortly.

Brings Horses cried, "Oh, can't we go on to the camp where the dancing is?"

Stormy was cross even to her. "We will do what the wise old men decide."

What was decided was confusion. Some of the refugees decided to go with Chief Hump, taking their women. They would surrender to the white soldiers. They rode away, yelling and angry.

Others, including Elk Rising's group and twenty of

225

Hump's young Miniconjou warriors, chose to go to Big Foot's camp. He was a great peacemaker, they proclaimed; besides, his people were still faithful to the Messiah and his sacred dance.

When they reached the ragged, temporary camp, there were some soldiers there, but not many. Big Foot was in council with the officers. One officer scolded him roundly for taking in the fleeing, hostile Hunkpapas, but the chief made them all proud with his answer:

"Of course I will take them in. There is nothing else I can do. These are my people, my brothers. They are starved and weary and almost naked. So I make room for them."

The Hunkpapas were welcomed, though with some fear, to the lodges of the Miniconjous, who were hungry themselves, and cold because they had not been able to go to their agency for their winter annuity of warm clothing and new blankets, and tired out because the soldiers had kept chasing them.

The refugees from Grand River had to be scattered through the camp, one person here, two there, wherever there was space and extra bedding. The Miniconjou women wanted to be good to the homeless, but they themselves were confused and very nervous, and in two lodges young women were in labor.

Elk Rising gathered his family together (except that Saved Her Cub had disappeared) and spoke: "We must find lodges for Brings Horses and Red Pipe at least, and be sure we know where they are. We men will look out for ourselves."

A Miniconjou woman came out of her lodge and told them, "We can take two if you have your own blankets.

There is little to eat, but you are welcome." She pointed at Brings Horses. "You come, and your man with you. Maybe my sister will take the young woman." She shouted, and a woman in the next lodge answered, "Yes, bring her."

The street of the camp was full of moving people, carrying things, making room. Before going into the lodge, Brings Horses asked pitifully, "How soon will we dance?"

An old hag with ragged white hair railed at her, mumbling for lack of teeth, but two burly, scolding daughters took her away. Brings Horses, close to tears, entered the lodge and said the right things to the busy hostess.

Saved Her Cub, who had been ranging out to get acquainted with other young men, appeared and said, "I have brought you a present, Father and Mother." He had with him a smiling youth of about fifteen, to whom he spoke: "These are my parents, Elk Rising and Brings Horses Woman. She was born an Oglala. Tell her who you are."

The youth, who wore a ghost shirt, replied, "My name is She Throws Him. My father is Morning Rider. We are Oglalas."

Brings Horses threw her arms around him and began to sob. When she could talk, she pleaded, "Take me to my brother."

But from the doorway a deep, remembered voice said, "Sister, I am here. And my woman, Young Bird, is with me."

Ah, the happy crying! The touching of hands to long-unseen faces, the repeating of "Yes, it is really you! You have changed some, not much."

Those of the younger generation were embarrassed at being stared at and turned around and admired and fondled as if they were children. None of them were children. The youngest was Morning Rider's son, She Throws Him, who had been in his cradle bag in that last really good summer that anyone remembered, the year 1876 by the white man's count, and now it was December of 1890.

The older ones grieved for those who were gone since last they met—all dead of white men's diseases made fatal by hunger.

The young people joined a little in the wailing, even Stormy's sister, Red Pipe Woman. She was often sullen, but now she remembered courtesy, and Stormy was proud of her.

All wore ghost shirts or dresses except Stormy and his mother; even Red Pipe Woman, who had never danced, wore the dress her mother had given her.

The younger ones slid out without being noticed, wanting to rest from the emotion. Brings Horses was asking frantically, "When will the dancing begin? We must dance. Because the time is short, and my mother told me in a vision, 'Meet me in the south.' "

Morning Rider came out to tell the younger ones, "You will all come to my lodge, and never mind if it is crowded. These good people here are crowded, too. Young Bird will go now to get things ready."

But they could not all go at once, because Brings Horses was telling the Miniconjou woman about her mother, Whirlwind, and how brave she had been, and the woman would not let her go until she heard it all. And about the vision: "Meet me in the south."

She was good to them, the Miniconjou. She, too, was a believer in the Dance of Spirits Returning and was anxious for the dancing to begin again.

"But the soldiers keep moving us, and Chief Big Foot hardly knows what to do," she complained. "Your brother and his wife have been with us a long time from Pine Ridge so they could dance with us. Tell me, why does Young Bird wear the bonnet with magpie wings? She never mentions it."

So Brings Horses explained: "When we were running to Canada, in the bitter winter, the soldiers attacked and burned our camp. Young Bird saved many things from our lodge when it was burning, and her face on one side was terribly burned, and all her hair on that side. So I made her the bonnet and the braid, and sometimes she uses different birds' wings on it. Ah, she is brave! She has suffered."

Outside, huddled together and shivering, the young people listened and were proud. Their young Oglala cousin, She Throws Him, said quietly, "I was in my cradle bag then, but I have heard the stories so often that it seems I was there and can remember."

"You *were* there," Stormy reminded him. "You were the baby that Grandmother Whirlwind saved from the she-grizzly that wounded her and crippled her. It is right that we all remember."

"And soon after the earth shakes," the boy mused, "when the Christ comes, and the buffalo herds and the ponies, and the spirits of all those who went before us, we will be with Grandmother Whirlwind. Think of it! . . . But Stormy, you do not wear the ghost shirt to protect you from the white soldiers' bullets. Why?"

"I have not danced," Stormy admitted. "I was working at the agency, and no dances were held there."

His brother Saved Her Cub threw off his blanket and stripped off his ghost shirt. "Give me your shirt, because it's cold," he said. "Now you can wear a ghost shirt, and my faith will protect me."

"No!" Stormy objected. Then he did as ordered. "Thank you, Brother," he said quietly.

Red Pipe spoke: "I am wearing my mother's ghost dress, but it is a lie. I have not danced. I will, as soon as we can."

They stopped talking then, hearing the enormous voice of the camp herald: "Ho, you people! The soldier chief has had many beeves killed because he knows we are hungry. They are being cut up now for a feast. Heads of families come to the chief's lodge to get meat!"

There was a happy cheer through the camp. People began to scurry around.

Stormy had been worrying about his sister; she drooped. "Maybe you should rest now," he suggested.

"I want to talk to you alone," she told him. "I have been thinking about something. But why should you be good to me? I am your bad sister."

"You are my sister. You have a hard life."

She began to cry a little.

"Come away from the fire and we'll sit down with my blanket around you, like a courting couple."

She laughed shortly. "How many courting couples are there among people who expect to be killed? But let us sit that way."

The other young people politely wandered off, with She Throws Him leading the way, to find White Mountain and carry their few possessions to the lodge of Morning Rider.

"I'll tell you something," Red Pipe Woman confided. "He was a white man, and he was going to marry me. I wanted to live like a white woman."

Stormy was startled. He replied rather formally, "I am glad you confide in me." She had not told even their mother.

"If we live through this, I will tell you his name," she said. "Then you can kill him for me." She smiled broadly, bitterly.

"I will do it," he promised. He wondered: What was the custom in the old days? They never told us any family stories about a problem like that, an unmarried woman pregnant. If a married woman gave herself to another man, her husband could cut off her nose; I remember a story about that. But what did a brother do if his sister . . . ? It doesn't matter. I have promised.

She had said, "If we live through this."

He sat beside her and casually laid his hand on her shoulder for comfort. He felt her go tense. He said in sympathy, "Red Pipe Woman, you are still young. It *was* better in the old days. It was according to established order. All the people knew what to do, the way their grandfathers had done things."

"Are you going to tell me it will be better in the future?" she asked suspiciously. "Of course. In the Land of Many Lodges."

He wanted to remove his hand but did not do it. He did not answer, either.

His sister went on talking, thinking. "You will be a great warrior there. I will know how to do a Lakota

231

woman's work, and live in a fine lodge that I made with my own hands. My man will be a Lakota man, a hunter, a proud warrior. But the oldest child in our lodge will not be his. It will be a half-white boy, growing tall, but my man will love him as much as his own."

Stormy said, "Yes."

His sister clutched his arm, suddenly frantic. "If all the whites are covered by mud when the earth shakes, will my baby boy be with us in spite of his white blood? Will he?"

"Of course," Stormy replied serenely. "Because he is half Lakota. There are many such."

Then she began to sob into her hands, sobbing hard. He thought it was good for her to have that release.

"Everything is going to be all right," he assured her.

He realized that his left hand, in his pocket, was clutching the rattles of the snake that was his medicine, although he had not believed it. Now he did. The rattles rustled dryly in his hand. He wished it had taught him a sacred song, but he remembered well, after all these years, the song he had made up. In a low voice he chanted it:

"The snake spirit looked at me, looked at me.
The sky sent a voice with a message.
It was cold on the hill top."

"What does that mean?" his sister whispered.

"I can't tell you that. It is a private sorrow," he answered.

He was not going to ask his Pine Ridge relatives whether his *kola* was dead. He knew without asking. He said, "I had a friend who said once, 'I want to ride a good spotted pony and wear feathers on my head.' He wears them now, and I will do that, too. I will teach my young nephew to ride well and shoot straight. And you will be proud of him. Your man, my brother-in-law, and I will teach him to be a great man. Even Grandmother Whirlwind will be proud of him. What will you name him?"

"That can wait," she said. "There is plenty of time. . . . You don't believe that, do you?" She sounded like the sullen sister he remembered, the one he did not really know.

Stormy thought hard. "Yes," he answered. "I believe it, because I must. We can't go back. We can only go ahead to the Land of Many Lodges. The sacred dance may hurry it up, that is all."

They began to walk in the direction their parents had gone, to the lodge of Morning Rider. On the way they met White Mountain, who said, "I was looking for you. Stormy, you have your gun? Of course. Keep it with you always, under your blanket. I think there will be trouble."

"So do I, but how do you know?"

"It is a stirring in the blood and among the people. You were too young to remember when these feelings used to have important meaning. But I remember. There is panic, although we hear no screams. I have been talking to other men—we would have been warriors in the long-ago time. They feel it too. And there is something bad: Chief Big Foot is not only old and tired, he is sick. He promised the soldier chiefs we would do as they said, but he will not be able to control the trouble. Now let us find your brother and tell him. Red Pipe, you should be with your mother."

She said, "All right," like an obedient woman, unlike the sulky sister who, only a few minutes earlier, had confessed to Stormy that she was bad.

The men roamed far in the camp, listening more than they talked. They saw where Big Foot's tent was—an army tent, that the soldiers had put up because he was sick—and heard snatches of conversation everywhere, rumors, really. Occasionally an Indian scout rode to the tent and dismounted. Important-looking Miniconjou head men went in and out. So did soldiers.

Then a soldier chief came out, with a half-blood interpreter and three other soldiers, and began issuing orders in English.

Stormy murmured to those near him: "Big Foot has promised to surrender. The soldier chief says more soldiers are coming. He says we must all turn back to Big Foot's permanent village tomorrow, and then go on past it."

White Mountain commented, "The women are cross and cold and angry. Men told me that in their permanent camp many of them have cabins, so they will be warmer. I would not want to be the chief to try to push those women out of their homes again, once they get into them!"

The women did calm down, when they learned they were going home. The night was quiet after the soldiers marched out to their bivouac, but in the ragged lodge of Morning Rider everyone stayed up late, because they had so much to talk about, the two families so long divided. In other lodges and in the cabins there was fretting, there were threats, the sounds of anger could be heard, but in Morning Rider's there was the joy of reunion after long separation.

Everybody talked, although the younger ones, the children of Morning Rider and of his sister, did not interrupt when their elders told stories of the old, good days, reminding the younger generation of their heritage of valor. They talked much of Grandmother Whirlwind.

"A brave woman, our mother," Morning Rider told Brings Horses Woman. "We guessed she was starving herself on the way to the Grandmother's Land, to Canada, when we had so little. She was giving us her strength. We could not give it back."

"And just before she died, my baby died," Brings Horses remembered, "and she comforted me by promising to take him all the way along the Spirit Road to the Land of Many Lodges, because he was so little, but she could find the way. Almost with her last breath she promised."

Elk Rising remarked thoughtfully, "He is growing tall there now, a little younger than She Throws Him here, and he will be a good man. Whirlwind will see to it. Her daughter, my woman, is brave, too. She carries a warrior's scar on her arm from a bullet wound that time we crossed south of the Medicine Line and brought back buffalo meat."

"It is nothing, nothing," Brings Horses insisted, hiding the old, puckered bullet scar. "You men shot the buffalo. All the women did was hurry the packhorses back with the meat. . . . And my brother's wife, with the bird's wings on the bonnet—ah, she was so brave when the soldiers burned our camp. She dared the fire to save food and blankets. We would have died without them."

"Sometimes," said Morning Rider, smiling, "I call her Pretty Wings."

Young Bird hid her scarred face in her hands.

They talked also of those who were absent, being dead.

"How soon will the sacred dance begin again?" Brings Horses asked pitifully. "After Stormy and Red Pipe dance, we will all be safe. Then we can all be together."

Her brother shook his head. "Not until after we get away to the Bad Lands, where Kicking Bear and the other dancers have gone."

He had no way of knowing that the hostiles in the Bad Lands had come out of their stronghold, had been persuaded to surrender.

It was a happy night in the lodge, everybody proud of everybody else, so many questions asked and answered! There was no talk of futures on the earth as they saw it now. They saw it as it would be. Even Stormy thought he could hear the thundering hoofs of the buffalo returning, and the hoofs of the thousands of ponies. He would ride a spotted pony and wear earned feathers on his head, and beside him, shouting and vigorous, would gallop that fine young man Takes Much, his *kola*.

17

"When Everything Is Gone . . ."

Next morning the soldier chief divided up all the people into three groups. Those who had horses rode them. Some young men, angry, wore face paint and cavorted in a threatening way before the soldiers. There were many old wagons to carry the horseless, and some pony drags for baggage and small children. One wagon got caught at a gate because the horses spooked, and all the people near it went into a panic. The young men raced their horses, brandishing rifles and shouting. But Chief Big Foot sent messengers to calm everyone, although he was now so sick that he was bleeding from his nose and spitting blood. He was lying in a wagon.

The soldier chief saw that he could not make them pass their own village without firing his big guns at them, so with Big Foot's promise of surrender he left them there and marched his own men to camp a few miles away. Now the Indian village buzzed like a chopped bee tree.

The weather was suddenly terrible—no snow, but a bitter wind that swirled sand and dry dust to make travel awful. The drought that Sitting Bull had promised had been going on for a desperately long time. Sand blew into the cloth lodge of Morning Rider, who had no cabin. The wind blew sparks from the fire to places where they should not go. Everybody was restless, disturbed, trying to keep warm, trying to keep cloth from catching fire.

"But we do not have to travel any more today," Brings Horses remarked with satisfaction.

Her brother shook his head. "I am afraid we do. I have a feeling in the blood and the bones, and the Miniconjous are talking. Listen."

They could indeed hear horses, men riding and calling, the sounds of anger.

"Big Foot cannot control them if they decide to go," he said, and the men in his crowded lodge agreed. "I think they may decide to head for the Bad Lands, for the place called the Stronghold where the angriest people went."

The people left before dawn, in spite of Big Foot's promise to the white soldier chief. He went with them, lying in a wagon, very sick, still arguing, but growing weaker.

For three days they eluded the pursuing soldiers, who were now moving in from all directions, searching that broken country for Big Foot.

Then, toward sunset, the Lakotas were captured with no trouble at all, and told where they must camp, beside a creek called Wounded Knee.

A soldier pointed and made the location very clear. Some of the young men with paint on their faces raced their horses around and waved rifles in a threatening way. The women were mostly very bad-tempered; they had been chivvied around too much lately, moved too often, become confused and nervous. The older men were silent, except a medicine priest named Yellow Bird who kept making threats. Children cried—sometimes because their mothers slapped them.

That was a bad thing, slapping. The Lakota women had learned it from the way white women treated their own children.

Stormy helped his mother and sister pitch what was left of their lodge—and that was not a Lakota thing to do, either. His sister reminded him of this fact. She looked sulky.

"What difference does it make?" he asked. "We have to help each other."

"It is not a thing for a Lakota man to do," she objected.

"And what should I be doing?" he asked with a wry smile.

She shrugged. "Nothing is any use, is it?"

"I don't know. But look at our mother's face."

Brings Horses Woman was utterly serene as she worked. There was a shining in her gaunt face.

Stormy said, "She has hope because she has faith. All she worries about is that we have never danced. Sister, pretend you are not afraid. That is what we can do."

He glanced at his father. That face had no expression at all. His father was watching the soldiers, who were on higher ground. They were setting up big guns or standing with rifles.

Elk Rising came over and remarked, "Do you see the little flags that some of the soldiers carry? Red and blue, with crossed knives on them and a number above the knives?"

"Yes, the number is 7," Stormy replied.

"We found little flags like that after the big fight we won at the Little Big Horn, many years ago," his father said. "I think these soldiers belong to the same warrior society. And now they will get even for that great defeat."

"Maybe the earth will shake first," Stormy told him, "and swallow them all up."

Elk Rising almost smiled. "Tell your mother that if she mentions the little flags."

Stormy stared up at a guidon of the Seventh Cavalry with its crossed sabers, not knowing those words, guidon and sabers, but remembering a ragged flag like that, seen in camp when he was a little boy.

He clutched his medicine snake rattles in his hand and began to sing in a low voice, walking away:

"The snake spirit looked at me, looked at me.
The sky sent a voice with a message.
It was cold on the hilltop."

That night they slept badly. Above them on the higher ground, some of the soldier chiefs were merry with a keg of whiskey.

Stormy awoke from scant sleep and a bad dream, shivering. A snake had been in his dream. He had been afraid —and he was stll afraid. There was nothing wrong with being afraid, though, as long as a man did not let it show. And he knew what the snake was. The Wasichus, the white men. All around them, on the ridges, ready to kill them.

He wished for a fleeting moment that he had stayed at

the agency, working like a slave at the trader's store, safe and dully married to Bright Water Woman. He put that shameful thought aside.

"This is where I belong," he told himself with pride. "With my family, whatever happens to us now."

Someone was stirring. He opened his eyes and saw that it was his mother, building a little fire. The wind was still blowing; everything he touched, including his face, had sand on it. He turned over cautiously, and his brother beside him looked at him with half a smile. They pulled their blankets around them and walked outside, stepping over people who still slept. The smell of other morning fires was in the air. On the ridges, too, the soldiers were cooking breakfast.

Outdoors, he asked Saved Her Cub, as they walked together, "Did you have a girl at Grand River?"

His brother said, with that sidewise glance and ready smile, "Of course. Am I so ugly that no girl would look at me?"

"You are," Stormy teased, "but some girls are not very particular. Did you think of marrying her?"

"I thought of it, but I didn't say anything. Any more than you did to your girl at the agency."

"Where is she now?"

"I don't know. We will never know, will we?"

"We think with one mind," Stormy told him. "So we do not have to talk about what is coming next. . . . I had a bad dream. About snakes."

"I had a good one," his brother confided. "About Grandmother Whirlwind. She told me something important."

Stormy was startled. "What did she tell you?"

241

"We think with one mind, so you should know," Saved Her Cub teased. "Therefore I do not need to tell you."

"I don't care what it was."

Saved Her Cub looked at him with mock pity, shaking his head. "You have been with forked-tongue white men too much. That is what makes you a liar."

Stormy laughed aloud. It was the only laughter in the dreary, waiting camp.

The camp crier, Wounded Hand, shouted through the village while it was still not daylight (for this was December 29 by the white man's calendar): "Family heads, come to Big Foot's tent for rations!"

The older men went to that place, up on a ridge. They could not talk to the chief, who was very sick now, but the soldiers had made him as comfortable as possible in an army tent with a small stove in it, and that was a good meeting place. They noticed, as they carried food to their homes, much marching of soldiers as the troops changed position on the ridges around the camp.

There was little talk at breakfast. Everybody just waited.

"We should keep our guns out of sight," Elk Rising murmured, so they put some of them under the bed places and the women sat down on the blankets, apparently resting.

She Throws Him, who had been roaming around as boys will do, and keeping his eyes and ears busy, slipped in with news: "They are going to take our guns away." His elders gasped. "But Big Foot says to bring out only the old ones, keep the good ones." He added, "I think an interpreter told the soldier chief what he said."

Morning Rider said grimly, "We will not give up the good guns!"

The big voice of Wounded Hand, the crier, sounded as he walked along: "Men, come to Big Foot's tent. The soldier chief wants to talk to us."

Even Saved Her Cub went with the others, although Young Bird protested, because he was so young. Morning Rider quieted her with a word. Who was to say that the boy was not a man?

They lined up, or bunched up, where they were told, and two of the Wasichu subchiefs counted off ten at each end and ordered them, through an interpreter, "Go to your homes and bring back all your guns."

The men walked in silence, in dignity. They returned to the soldiers. All twenty handed over only two guns among them, both old and not much good. The Wasichus muttered.

The Wasichus conferred; then they had sick old Big Foot carried out of the tent, weak and bleeding from the nose. They laid him on the ground. His head men gathered behind him and sat down.

Meanwhile, someone barked orders, and soldiers were marching around into other positions.

The soldier chiefs had an argument with Big Foot, who could barely speak.

"They have no guns," he insisted. "They turned the guns over to soldiers at the agency, and the guns were all burned up."

So the Wasichu chiefs decided to search the lodges where the women were. Plain soldiers went along, but only officers entered the lodges and searched there. They even picked up seated women, who fought them, screaming, and made the listening Lakota men, up on the ridge, very anxious—and under the bedding found good guns.

Plain soldiers searched baggage outside the lodges. They took axes and bows and arrows, hatchets, even knives—tools without which the people could not live at all.

Old Yellow Bird, the angry medicine priest, kept roaming around, chanting and advising, reminding the people that the ghost shirts made them immune to bullets, that the earth would shake soon.

When all the lodges had been searched, there were thirty-eight rifles, a few of them good ones. That was not nearly enough to satisfy the soldiers.

The tense Lakota men had been milling around considerably. The soldiers were equally tense, their rifles ready.

Stormy saw that his father was cautiously sidestepping into a position where he would have a better view of their lodge. The male relatives moved with him, trying to seem casual, wanting not to be noticed by the watchful soldiers.

Down among the lodges, many women had come out to watch. Stormy saw Young Bird and Red Pipe Woman. Was his mother still inside? Good—but the coarse cloth wall of the lodge would not turn aside a bullet.

Yellow Bird, the medicine priest, was dancing now, praying in a monotonous chant, stopping sometimes to remind the Lakotas that their ghost shirts would ward off the Wasichus' bullets and the earth would shake.

An order came through an interpreter: "Lakota men, come forward and open your blankets!"

The medicine priest stooped and picked up a handful of dirt, hurled it toward the soldiers, yelling to his people, "Do not be afraid! Let your hearts be strong!"

A few old men obeyed the officer's order. They opened their blankets. They had no guns. The soldiers began to force some young men to pass the officers. Two of the first three had good rifles. All the rest began to stir, keyed up, excited.

The soldiers were in separate lines, some in position to guard their own tent camp, others facing other ways, facing soldiers some distance away, or the Indians' camp or the Indian men.

Stormy could see that, if it came to a fight, soldiers might shoot at other soldiers and the Lakotas might be firing right into their own camp if their shots missed soldiers. Strange, but that was how the soldiers had been ordered to stand. It was bad for everybody.

A Lakota man suddenly waved a rifle above his head, shouting that he had paid much money for the gun and would not give it up. Two soldiers grabbed him from behind and the rifle fired. At that moment, Yellow Bird threw another handful of dirt into the air.

Half a dozen young Lakota men tossed back their blankets and leveled rifles that had been concealed, aiming at the soldiers. They fired, and tense soldiers fired back.

There was no time to race down to protect the women. Stormy and his male relatives fired at soldiers, fired fast with their good repeating rifles.

Crouching, reloading the magazine, Stormy glanced down at the lodge.

On the ground beside it, two women had fallen. He glimpsed a cap with magpie wings near one of them. The other had lost her shawl. She wore a ghost dress. *Ah, my sister!* She was trying to move.

Where is my mother?

In all the noise, Stormy heard a man behind him grunt—his father? Wounded?

Stormy fired carefully and saw soldiers go down. There was much shooting. Everybody shooting. Some screaming.

Reloading again, Stormy glanced toward the tattered lodge. His mother came crawling, hampered by her blanket. She stopped for an instant when a bullet hit her, then crawled again toward Red Pipe Woman.

Stormy was knocked sideways by a bullet in the right shoulder. His gun fell from his hands. In anguish that was not yet physical pain, he stared at the women. His mother lay partly covering his sister with her own body. Neither of them moved.

Meet me in the south.

Stormy felt a tremendous blow in the belly that knocked the wind out of him. The blow pushed him backward onto somebody, and he lay looking upward, feeling blood pump out.

Suddenly someone lay partly across him—his father, trying to protect him?

All around there was firing, some of it from big guns. The shouts and screams, the rage and terror did not concern him. He could not move. That did not matter. The ghost shirt his brother had given him had not protected him. They were all dead, he thought, and he was going, but he did not care about the pain or the blood that was draining out of him.

Dying was easy. He seemed to be floating on a cloud.

I want to wear feathers on my head and ride a good spotted pony.

Whatever happened was going to be all right. He was not sorry about anything. He was with those he loved, those who had loved him. All dead or dying now. But the earth was moving as had been promised. His mother's faith was true.

He heard someone moan—the boy, She Throws Him?—and tried to say, for comfort, "I see the buffalo coming," but no words came out.

Drifting on his cloud or on the moving earth, he seemed to be seeing the face of an old woman he did not remember very well. She spoke earnestly, his grandmother Whirlwind:

"When everything is gone, there is still love. That is how we lived. That is what matters."

He whispered, "Yes."

The gunfire continued, but he did not hear it.

A blizzard howled for two days, with bitter wind but little snow. It was January 1, 1891, when a bunch of Lakotas and white soldiers and thirty white civilians returned to Wounded Knee. Under three inches of snow they found utter horror of frozen, shattered, contorted bodies—and a few babies still alive. While the Lakotas searched for wounded living and identified their dead and roared their grief, the white civilians gathered the bodies and piled them up and dug a great pit. (And stripped some of the useless ghost shirts and dresses off for keepsakes, because the dead could as well go into the pit naked.)

One of the civilians made a careful count of Indian bodies, because the contract with the military called for payment of two dollars for each of those buried. He counted 102 adult men and women, 24 old men, 7 old women, 6 boys between five and eight years, and 7 babies under two. (There were many more who died after crawling away to hide, but they were not found until later.)

The workmen, knowing how many bodies they would be paid for, a total of 146, pushed them all into the big pit, had their photograph taken, and shoveled dirt in to fill the hole.

The white soldiers lost one officer and 24 enlisted men killed, 39 wounded. Three officers and 15 enlisted men received Medals of Honor for heroism in the Battle of Wounded Knee.

Wovoka, who had brought the sacred dance from heaven, lived in Nevada until 1932. His people mourned the passing of a medicine priest, but the local newspaper did not even notice. He was known by the white-man name of Jack Wilson, and he was thought to be seventy-four.